Dog Food 2:

K'wan Presents

Dog Food 2:

K'wan Presents

Raynesha Pittman

www.urbanbooks.net

Urban Books, LLC
97 N18th Street
Wyandanch, NY 11798

Dog Food 2: K'wan Presents
Copyright © 2016 Raynesha Pittman

ISBN 13: 978-1-62286-733-2
ISBN 10: 1-62286-733-5

First Mass Market Printing December 2016
Printed in the United States of America

10 9 8 7 6 5 4 3 2 1

This is a work of fiction. Any references or similarities to actual events, real people, living or dead, or to real locales are intended to give the novel a sense of reality. Any similarity in other names, characters, places, and incidents is entirely coincidental.

Distributed by Kensington Publishing Corp.
Submit Orders to:
Customer Service
400 Hahn Road
Westminster, MD 21157-4627
Phone: 1-800-733-3000
Fax: 1-800-659-2436

Dog Food 2:

K'wan Presents

Raynesha Pittman

Dedication

When my fire burned out, it was your love that ignited the flame. When I felt like I couldn't finish the race, it was your cheers that pushed me to reach the checkered flag. And when the world made it hard for me to breathe, it was your smiling faces that gave me oxygen.

To my six beautiful children, my loving husband, my always supportive mother, and my family who truly knows the meaning, both blood and mud. To my publisher and his lovely wife, who believed in me when others wouldn't give me a chance. To the authors, who have consistently given me encouraging words and advice. To my best friend, who throws a cookout for me in my sunshine and provides an umbrella in my storms, and to the readers who took a chance on me by picking up my book(s), I dedicate this one to all of you.

Dedication

There are no words that can adequately express what all of you mean to me, but please know I'm thankful to each and every one of you. Smile, my loves. This one is for you!

—Author Raynesha Pittman

Prologue

The boat was overcrowded with Haitian professionals and their families, eager to embrace a new beginning in America, because Papa Doc had allowed the power that came along with being elected president to go to his head. He had become a dictator faster than an eye could blink and he went to the extreme of declaring himself president for life. He'd even gone as far as changing the island's flag and colors to ones that put the focus on what mattered to him most: himself. His first act as ruler was to take away the rights previously given to Haitian citizens by past rulers. He'd made the educated his first targets of political persecution. Those who were on the boat were fed up with his reign of terror and his secret police's deadly enforcement of it. Feeling hopeless, they'd packed up, falsified documents, and headed to America for permanent residency and political asylum.

Homemade flasks filled to capacity with the finest wines the island produced were held in the air as they made toast after toast while a radio no bigger than a man's shoe played American soul music. Some had never heard of Motown and its musicians, but that didn't stop them from snapping their fingers to the contagious beats. Although freedom was still a few hours away, for most true freedom came when their boat wasn't destroyed as they made their departure from Haiti.

Franco Sr. and his brother Jean Paul had heard talk of the one-way trip to freedom from one of the college professors Papa Doc had sent them to dispose of. It had been rumored that the professor and a few of his colleagues were plotting to assassinate Papa Doc, so Papa Doc had to ensure that those making the plans were terminated like the rodents he felt they were. There wasn't any proof to support the claims but, knowing the level of hate the majority of the citizens had for him, Papa Doc took all rumors at face value.

Franco began his torture session by slowly piercing with his dull knife the flesh that protected the professor's heart from exposure to the world. As he did this, he received all the details about the voyage. It wasn't until he watched his brother sear the dead educator's head off his neck that he realized that they needed to be on that boat. Franco was done playing wolf to the sheep, and Papa Doc's glamour had long faded from Franco's eyes. He knew his days of being a loyal follower of the president would bring death to visit him before his time. America would provide the safety he and his family would need after he'd sealed his fate by supporting the bloody regime. Getting on that boat wouldn't be a problem; but convincing his brother to join him would be Franco's greatest challenge.

"Why does he always ask for their heads?" Jean Paul asked as he closed the eyes on his prey and stuffed his head into the shit-brown sack he carried on his bare, muscular shoulders.

"You don't know? He thinks he's God, and li pa mete konfyans nou," Franco said to his younger brother, switching the conversation from broken English to their native tongue.

"Why do you say he doesn't trust us, brother? He sends us on his most important missions because he has faith we will accomplish them. You are becoming like one of the men we hunt with the disloyalty you speak carelessly in your words."

"My loyalty doesn't belong to him; it lies with you and my sons," Franco retorted. "Not even

the women in our family deserve it. Our wives don't bleed our blood, and our daughters will choose to marry out of it. Don't speak to me about my disloyalty, brother, when we are working for the most disloyal of them all."

"I won't listen to your blasphemy, Franco. Your way of thinking will land your head in this sack."

"And your faith, baby brother, in our island's biggest traitor will make you the disloyal one who carries it."

Jean Paul's walk turned into a stride as he made his way back to the Jeep, leaving his brother behind in the decaying gingerbread house. Franco had to admire the heart his brother held in his guerrilla-shaped chest. It was the heart of their mother, and that same heart had caused her to be raped and murdered in front of the boys.

Edith, as the islanders called her, opened her home to a wounded hurricane victim and spent long hours nursing him back to health. Once the stranger healed, he repaid her by sexually assaulting her and taking his blade from her stomach to her chin. The boys were small children when it happened and they were still mourning the loss of their father, who had recently gone missing, so neither brother ran to her defense. They sat, frozen in fear, as their mother was slaughtered like a wild boar.

With the loss of the only parent they had left, Franco inherited the role of protector and provider. He quickly moved them out of the shack their father had built with his own hands and into the island's brushy backyard for shelter. They had spent many nights without food, but they had each other and, in the boy's eyes, that was all that really mattered.

Over the years, the brothers were taken in by many families, but Franco only allowed them to stay with the surrogates long enough to save enough money and food to flee, so they could continue to live together alone. Franco had spent many sleepless nights watching his younger brother sleep in the tall grass the island provided while daydreaming about the future—not of his own future, but of the foundation he was building for his brother to ensure he had a fruitful one. He didn't care what became of himself or if he hungered. As long as Jean Paul was taken care of, he was at peace. Franco mixed and laid the concrete of his brother's future with education. No matter where they were or what they had been through throughout the day, Jean Paul wasn't allowed to rest until he'd completed a lesson out of the schoolbook Franco had stolen from their last surrogates.

It must have been voodoo that allowed the boys to be welcomed into the home of an aging history teacher and his wife. Yann made it a priority to spend four hours a day teaching the boys at home after teaching his students,. He loved them and took to them quickly. He felt God had given him the children his infertility had prevented him from having.

It broke Franco's heart when they had to leave, but Yann's wife, Nadia, didn't leave him a choice. At the time, the eight-year-old had become accustomed to fulfilling the wife's sexual needs while her husband worked. She was tired of going unsatisfied due to her husband's impotency and she found what she was lacking from Yann in the pants of the little boy she publically called her son.

It began with her bathing Franco like many of the island's women did their children, but Nadia, then, would pay too much attention to his genital area. She boldly replaced the washrag and soap with her tongue and saliva. She never cared about the pain she caused the child by using her mouth to grow his underdeveloped meat; she put her needs first. Once Nadia had mastered getting him erect, she upgraded him to penetrating her virgin-like womb. Sex with Franco made it easier for her to stay married to a man who lacked everything that separated him from being a woman.

Franco allowed their sexual relationship to go on for a year, and he would have allowed it to continue, but his new mother's and lover's eyes fell on a new prey when Jean Paul turned eight. Franco wouldn't allow his brother to experience the mental and physical strain he was battling, so his manhood instincts kicked in. Three was more than a crowd to Franco; it was a village. So he packed them up and left before she could have her way with his younger brother. Jean Paul questioned him for many days after their departure, but all Franco would say was, "I promised you a better life, and I'm going to give it to you."

They were of age now and had families of their own, but Franco still felt the need to make good on his promise. He knew America would present him that opportunity and more.

Franco had just finished filling his sack with the riches of the professor's home when his brother walked back in. "What is taking you so long? We are already a day behind schedule, and I'm sure he has sent his men to look for us. Let's go, now!"

Franco tied up his sack and followed his brother out of the house out of respect, not *fear. They both shared the body frames of fully grown guerrillas. Franco's was half a foot taller than Jean Paul's and he was the color of heated brown sugar coated in honey; and Jean Paul, standing at five feet eight inches, looked as if he had swum in coffee grinds. Both boys were handsome and built for whatever life would throw at them.*

Jean Paul was still upset, and Franco could tell by the dashes his once big brown eyes had turned into, so he decided to ride in silence to let his brother's anger vanish on its own. Many moments passed before Jean Paul broke their silence.

"Brother, do you see that?" Jean Paul asked, now standing up on the passenger's side of the Jeep, pointing at the trees a quarter of a mile ahead of them. "The smoke is coming from your house. Drive faster."

Franco stepped on the gas to show he agreed. Both brothers knew their families were in the house, awaiting their return. They prayed they would find them standing outside, waiting for them safely, but that wasn't to be the case. Instead, they pulled up to an armed guard standing in front of the blaze.

Franco jumped out the Jeep before it came to a complete stop. "What is this? Where is my family?" Franco shouted at the smiling guard.

"The next time Papa Doc gives you a deadline, you should stick to it."

Jean Paul didn't wait for more information. He quickly subdued the henchman by snapping his neck and then he ran into the house with Franco on his heels. There wasn't a need for the brothers to move past the living room because in a pile, stacked like dirty laundry, were both of their families. Each had a single bullet wound in the head.

"No!" Jean Paul screamed as he picked up his youngest son's body. He cradled him like the infant he was and he carried his lifeless body out of the burning house. Franco watched, frozen. He wasn't afraid of death; his fear was of death taking the lives of those he loved.

"Franco! Help me, brother. We shall bury them. Their flesh will not mix with the ashes of this house."

Franco still didn't make a move.

"Brother, do you hear me?" Jean Paul shouted, but it fell on deaf ears.

Franco had checked out. His mind was no longer on the loss of his family and the home he had built for them; it was on the boat to freedom. As Jean Paul ran out with Franco's wife's body, Franco grabbed the henchman by the ankles and dragged him into the house.

"What are you doing?" Jean Paul was beyond frustrated with his brother, and he couldn't deal with his crazy way of thinking right now. He wanted a quick answer from Franco and, when he didn't get it, he continued to remove the bodies like he had never said a word. As fast as Jean Paul could pull them out the house, Franco was bringing the bodies back in.

Instead of questioning his brother, Jean Paul attacked him inside the burning house. Neither brother threw a balled fist at the other, but their wrestling was just as dangerous, as shards of the house began to fall around them. Too occupied with their fight, the brothers didn't realize that, if they didn't stop, death would return for them.

"Stop it!" a prepubescent voice yelled.

As if time had been stopped at the words, both brothers came to a halt and glanced at the figure standing in the doorframe.

"We must leave! The people you work for are approaching from the north."

Franco Jr. had a fully packed sack on his back and was standing in the door covered in smoke. He had escaped the house with his oldest sister before their family's execution. His sister, Melyssa, had urged him to flee the area with her, but he'd refused and hidden in a tree, *awaiting his father and uncle's return. Both men were excited to see him and rushed to him as he said, "I will tell you everything once we get away from here, Father. Follow me."*

"I'm not leaving my family, nephew. The men who did this will die by my hands at the same place they took my family from me," Jean Paul said as bitter tears fell.

"Then, you stay here, Uncle, and die with those you love. Father, we must go."

Franco was surprised at how much strength his ten-year-old had shown. There wasn't a sign of sorrow on his face; his look was of a man who was determined. Franco Sr. had spent many nights exposing his firstborn son to the real world, against his wife's constant protests, and those lessons were showing at that very moment; but he couldn't leave his brother for dead.

"Jean Paul, if you want us to stand here and fight these men to the death, we can turn back to back and die side by side, together. But I made you a promise for a better life, and I intend to keep it. Where does your loyalty lie, my brother? With the men who took our families from us or with me in America?"

Jean Paul and Franco Jr. replied in unison, "America?"

"Yes, America. The land of the brave and the home of the free."

Jean Paul shook his head at his older brother and let out the laugh he had tried hard to hold back. Wrapping an arm around his nephew, he said, "It's the land of the free and the home of the brave. Lead us to freedom, my brother."

The Past

Chapter 1

Omar

When the Greyhound passed the WELCOME TO KENTUCKY sign on the 65-North to Louisville, the bullshit finally hit me. I had been exiled from Memphis by a crew of pussies. Their leaders were an old-ass drag queen and his son, the princess. I'd let them hoes give me my walking papers without making them sweat their makeup off or catch a run in their stockings. My focus was on self-preservation, never realizing I was in a game of pussy and about to be fucked. Only the weather understood the anger I was feeling as I looked out the dirty bus window at the lightning gangsta walking through the gray sky.

I tried to take a nap to sleep off the funk I was in. The goal was to wake up clear minded, ready to construct the blueprint of my next move. But the fucked-up shocks on the bus made me feel every bump as we exited the interstate, cutting my two-hour nap short. Realizing we were about to make a food stop, I dug in my pockets.

"Twenty punk-ass dollars! These niggas put me on a bus from Memphis to Detroit with nothing but pocket lint."

I flipped the two ten-dollar bills in my hand, hoping the movement would cause the mother-fuckas to multiply. I concentrated on the United States' first secretary of the treasury and his identical twin. I didn't realize I was talking out loud.

"Shit. I'll take it if you don't want it, youngster. You see that intersection up there? We're about to stop at that burger joint, and there's a liquor store that would gladly accept them dead presidents for a bottle of gin."

"Man, take your drunk ass back to sleep. Hamilton wasn't a president, and you don't need shit else to drink. You got liquor sweating out your pores."

The old cat was 'sleep when I got on the bus in Memphis and, since the bus was overcrowded, I had squeezed past his legs and sat next to him. I hadn't noticed he was passed out drunk until thirty minutes into the ride when he adjusted in his seat, and I got my first whiff of liquor.

"President or not, the nigga spends like one."

With his last words came the smell of old beer combined with vomit and a hint of morning breath. The mixture hit my nose like old farm animal shit and caused my empty stomach to bust a flip. I vowed not to inhale from my nose until I found another seat but, before I could, I got a whiff of something else less friendly.

"What the fuck is that smell? Did you pee on yourself, nigga?"

The old cat looked around as if he was sure I was talking to someone else.

"I'm talkin' to yo' ass! Man, you better scoot your pissy ass over before I fuck you up!"

"Who are you puttin' on a show for, tryin' to talk all loud and shit? I ain't pee on myself. That's water! I spilled it before you got your big mouth ass on the bus. You better deflate your chest, young nigga, because I ain't the one you wanna fuck with." He flashed the gun he had in the pocket of his black leather jacket as the bus came to a stop at the rest area.

"Don't show it unless you plan to use it," I said, standing to get off the bus and stretch my legs. "When I get back on this motherfucking bus, your drunk ass better have found yourself a new seat, pissy."

"Naw, I'm good right where I'm at. If you got a problem, you can move, President Hamilton."

I mugged him for a second, and then stepped in the aisle to let his ass off the bus first. I didn't care about the other passengers' complaints about me blocking the aisle. I wasn't going to give the cat the opportunity to sneak me from behind. After giving him the once-over and checking out his khaki-colored Dickies and high-top black Chuck Taylors with the fat laces outwardly laced, I didn't make my exit from the bus until I watched his old California gangsta ass walk across the street and into the liquor store. If he sat his seven-cornrows-with-no-hang-time-wearing ass back in the seat next to me when we got back on the bus, I'd wait until he fell back to sleep; then I'd whoop his ass and take his gun.

I made it inside the burger joint without incident and checked out the menu to put something on my stomach. I normally didn't fuck with food that could be cooked in under one minute, but this wasn't a normal situation. I hadn't eaten or drunk anything but the blood draining backward from my busted nose with a side of spit, and that was before I got evicted from Memphis.

"Umm, can I help you?"

When I looked up, my eyes told my brain to say, "Hell naw, bitch. I'm straight!" because her crossed eyes and yellow teeth made my stomach replicate the reaction from smelling the old cat's breath. But thanks to having a smoked-out pimp for an uncle, I said, "Yeah, beautiful, let me get a dollar chicken sandwich with no lettuce or those little crumbs y'all call onions. And let me get a large fry and a cold drink with that."

"What kind of cold drink?" she asked with a giggle.

"Whichever one you decide you want to give me for free, sweetheart."

I glanced at her name plate that was pinned on her shirt. It read UNIQUE. It was the perfect name for an ugly girl. It supplied an answer if she ever had the gall to ask if she was pretty. All you'd have to say was that she had a unique beauty and leave the conversation at that.

She dug under the counter and pulled out a large cup. "Will that be all, sir?"

"No, Unique. Can I get your number so we can stay in touch, too?"

She smiled like I knew she would, and I got a glimpse of her overlapping teeth at the top and the bottom of her gums. "I can't give you my number while I'm working, but thank you."

She giggled again, sounding sexy and girly, which didn't match her rough, boyish appearance. Her afro was even manly. It looked like she got her hair done in Detroit by the same bitch who did Ben Wallace's of the Pistons. Then, she continued by saying, "Your total is $4.47, handsome."

"All right." I forced a smile onto my face. I rubbed all my pockets from the outside of my jeans. I touched the left side of my chest to give the impression that my money might have been placed in my shirt pocket, but I was wearing a muscle shirt. My white T-shirt had my blood on it from Demarcus making my nose leak, plus whatever had spilled on my back when I was in the trunk of the car, so I threw that bitch in the trash at the Greyhound station back in Memphis.

"Damn, baby! I think I left my wallet on the bus!"

"The bus?" She screwed up her face, making herself even uglier, which I didn't think was possible. "You're on the city bus?"

"Hell naw!" I reached inside my pants pocket, pushed the cash and my driver's license to the side, and pulled out my Greyhound ticket. "I'm on the Greyhound, baby. Go ahead and cancel my order." I tried to sound frustrated and exhausted. "I've been riding since Memphis, and that long-ass bus ride has me slipping. But it was nice meeting you with your sexy ass."

I turned on my feet and faced the door. I put on a show for her one more time as I rechecked my pockets in disbelief.

"Where are you riding the Greyhound to?" she asked, while taking a full look at my body.

The rain had eased up from when we first entered Kentucky, but the drizzle had my arms and shoulders glistening. "I'm headed to Detroit for a while."

"So you're going to ride all the way to Detroit without eating? You just made it to Louisville; you still have a long way to go. Grab your wallet off the bus and come back!"

"I can't. The bus driver went on break too."

She checked her watch and then looked back at me. While licking the cracked and ashy balloons she called lips, she said, "How long is your layover? If you can wait ten minutes, I'll feed you." Then, she handed me the cup. "The drink fountain is over there. I'll bring you your food when it's ready."

Fifteen minutes later, I had a supersized meal with a bag full of road snacks and I was getting my dick sucked in the back seat of her Grand Prix a block from her job. I was munching on my fries when my swimmers were ready to swan dive down her throat, but she stopped bobbing.

"I want to sit on it!"

"You can't." My mouth was full, but she understood me. I locked my hands in her nappy afro and tried to return her mouth to my meat.

"Why not? He wants me."

I swallowed everything left in my mouth without chewing it to ensure she heard me. "Naw, he wants that throat. Besides, I don't have a condom."

She jumped up, climbed over the seat, and grabbed her purse off the passenger side floor. She went through it frantically until she found what she was looking for. "I got a condom!"

I had prayed she wouldn't find one, but she did. To my surprise, the Man Upstairs heard my prayer; but He must have been too busy to answer it at that moment. He made it up to me by letting the ring of the rubber slide out of the package and hit the floor as she held it up in the air.

"That bitch is open, and it's dried out. I'm not using that!"

I handed her the condom after I retrieved it from the floor. The disappointment that she wore was priceless. I grabbed her ugly ass by her waist and pulled her closer to me.

"Come here, beautiful." With my left hand, I forced her to lay her head on my chest as my meat deflated. "Look. He's mad at you now," I said, pointing at my lap. "Finish hooking me up with that mouth, and I'll play with the pussy."

"It's cool!" she said with an attitude present in her voice. "You don't have to. I'm kind of on my period anyways."

"Fuck you mean you're 'kinda on your period'!" I mushed the trifling ho in her face, forcing her to get the fuck off of me, and then I put my meat back in my pants.

"Not like that!" she snapped back. "It's my last day, so it's a little red still but not a lot. Don't try to play me like I was going to give it to you while my shit was flowing!"

I visualized myself knocking the bitch out with a quick combo. She wouldn't be the first bitch I'd had to put to sleep, nor would she be the last. With the intent to cause bodily harm written all over my face, I said, "Bitch, you're foul!" and jumped out of her whip, leaving her to watch me walk off from her back seat.

I hit a few blocks on her ass and then walked to the liquor store with the $150 in cash and the blank seventy-five dollar money order I'd stolen out of her purse while she lay on my chest. I grabbed myself a bottle of Rémy, took a long, hard swallow of it, and then introduced Alexander Hamilton to his new presidential company.

I stayed ducked off in the liquor store until I saw my bus loading. I didn't know if the bitch was going to turn up with the police looking for me, and I wasn't about to take any chances. I was the last to board, and the drunken nigga was still sitting in the same spot, smiling big at me. I scanned for an empty seat, but there wasn't one available, so I squeezed past his legs to retake my window seat. I made sure to give him a sharp elbow to his dome as I passed him.

"You did that shit on purpose," he said, holding the part of his forehead that rested in between his eyes.

"I never said I didn't! What'cha want to do about it? I'm not about to rap with you."

"Don't sleep on me, nigga! I wasn't trying to peace treaty with you by changing my clothes. That damn dog at my first layover must've peed on me, so I took that bullshit off. That weak shit you're on will get you fucked up. Keep your motherfucking hands to yourself if you plan to walk off this bus and not be carried off by the coroner's office in a body bag. Matter fact, don't say shit else to me!" He turned his back like an offended woman and even crossed his arms over his chest.

"Say no more, pissy!"

About a half bottle of Rémy later and whatever the fuck he was drinking, me and the old cat, whose name was L'Amir, were laughing, joking, and chopping shit up. When we made it to Detroit, I felt like I had known him all my life.

"Get a pen, youngsta, and jot down my number. I can't promise you that my boss will plug you in, but I'll definitely set up a meet-and-greet so he can feel you out."

"Thanks. All I need is for you to drop a good word with your plug, and I'll handle the rest."

L'Amir was shaking his head before I could complete my sentence. "Naw, I'm not vouching for shit. A bus ride and some conversation over liquor ain't enough for me to do all that, but I will point you in the direction of money. It'll be up to you after that, playa."

"I respect that."

I took his number; we shook it up, and then we went walking in our separate directions. I didn't have a plan, but hanging at the bus station wasn't one of them. I was tipsy, and formulating a plan wasn't something I needed to do at the moment. I caught the short end of a woman's cigarette and headed to the taxi pickup area. A motel, shower, and bed were all I needed for the night.

"Ay, Omar! You need a ride somewhere?" L'Amir pulled up on me, sitting on the passenger's side of a big white GMC SUV. He had a beautiful mixed thick chick driving him. She looked too young to be his old lady but too old to be his daughter.

"Yeah, I need to get dropped off at an extended stay or a cool motel where I can crash for a few days until I figure out my next move."

He hit the unlock button on the doors. "Get in, youngsta. We got you. This is my baby sister, Symphony. Symphony, that's my boy Omar. He's moving here from Memphis."

"Nice to meet you, Miss Symphony. What do people call you for short?"

She didn't return the greeting. She just stared at me with curiosity written all over her pretty face. What I couldn't make out was if the curiosity came from a positive or negative place.

"There you go, acting like Daddy. That man spoke to you, Symphony; you can, at least, say something back. Damn!" L'Amir snapped at his sister.

Her mouth never opened, so I fastened my seat belt in the seat behind hers. She continued to look at me through her rearview mirror. With a voice as deep and sultry as Toni Braxton's and Anita Baker's, she said, "If you just moved here, why don't you have any bags?"

Those words rolled off her tongue so beautifully that, for a second or two, I thought she had sung them to me. But, in those same seconds, I knew she was one of those pretty, smart-mouth bitches who would put a nigga through hell and back with her arguing. She didn't even give me time to answer before she started shooting off more questions to put in the profile she was building of me.

"How old are you? Do you have family here? If you do, why do you want to get dropped off at a motel? Are you hiding from somebody? And why are you wearing a muscle shirt and no jacket? It's freezing here!"

L'Amir took a deep breath, took out a cigarette, and fired it up.

"Ay, bruh. Let me get one of those too!" I said.

He reached back to hand me his pack, and Symphony sat up taller in her seat to show that she was mugging me through her mirror. "Are you going to answer me or what, Omar? If that is indeed your true name."

"Damn, girl! You calling me a liar and you don't know shit about me!" I snapped back.

"See. That's the thing. I don't know shit about you, and my brother has a history of picking up those who shouldn't be trusted as friends." She cut the engine off in the SUV and hit the unlock button on her doors before she continued. "Oh, and I never called you a liar. You let that leak out of your own mouth!"

I was in a losing battle, and L'Amir wasn't saying shit to help me out. I needed the ride but fuck the twenty-one questions. I opened the door and took my seat belt off.

"Yeah, you're hiding a lot of shit. Get back in the car, fugitive. If my brother says we're dropping you off, then that is what we're doing!" She lifted up the center console, pulled out her heat, and set it on her lap. "Don't make any fast moves with your country ass. My nerves are real bad, and I don't trust you for shit!"

I tapped L'Amir on the shoulder. "Man, what's up with your sister?"

He started making cat and dog fighting noises and then said, while laughing, "She must like you, youngsta. You're still alive!"

After he said that, all I could wonder was, *who in the fuck did I jump in the car with?*

The Present

Chapter 2

Demarcus

I gripped the rim of the toilet and ripped it to the porcelain god. I had called Earl twice, and he'd come running to my aid both times. My stomach was fucked up, and there wasn't a damn thing I could do about it. There wasn't a drink on the market that could calm my rattled nerves besides liquor and, with my face in the shitter, that was the last thing I needed to drink right now. I hadn't figured out what disgusted me the most: the weakness of my stomach due to the murder I had committed or the little splashes of shit water that hit my face from inside the truck stop's toilet. Whatever the cause was for my disgust really did not matter because the deed of killing Orlando was done. The battle was fought, and we had suffered a few causalities, but the mission was accomplished, and I had won.

I·had dreamed of shooting Orlando's head off his shoulders for three long years and, although my dreams didn't come true, I'd settled for the bullet I'd put through the back of his head. He wasn't the first man I'd had to kill, but he was the most important. While Rico, Spank, and a couple of my pops's goons took out his stash houses, Killa, JP, and I caught Orlando leaving the club. His whole style had changed into his brother Gutta's, but, even in Gutta's dying days, Orlando couldn't outdress him. His cockiness decreased the value of everything he had on. He made the Armani suit look like it had come from one of those "three suits for $199" stores, and he'd turned the shiny new gators he had on his feet into backyard lizards.

Our initial plan was to stay low. Our black hoodies and werewolf masks were to ensure just that, but Orlando's cockiness had caused me to come out of costume when he laughed at us.

"Look at this shit, Tay. These young niggas trying to rob us in their cheap-ass Dollar Tree masks. What are y'all trying to get, some Jordan money and a couple of dollars for some weed? Here. Take this funky-ass two hundred dollars I was going to blow my nose with and get the fuck out my face before y'all piss me off. Let's bounce, Tay."

Killa snatched the money out of Orlando's hands. Simultaneously, I snatched the mask off my face. "Naw, we're here to collect a little more than money from you. We already got back all the money you owe me."

Orlando's smile cracked and, for a second, he revealed the fear he had within on his extra baby-oiled face. I was glad I had caught his look, but I wasn't the only one who did.

"What's good, Orlando? You straight?" his boy Tay asked.

"Yeah, I'm good. I'm real good! What's up with you, Demarcus? You finally grew the balls to try to run up on me in Nashville, I see. I waited for you to come for a long-ass time. Then, I remembered how much of ho you are," he said, laughing. "So you robbed me? I take it you ran through my stash houses and my gas station, right? Nigga, your moves are so predictable!" He chuckled.

My mouth wouldn't open; anger had sealed it shut. I managed to nod my head once.

"We hit your baby mama's house, too, and the parking garage you keep them clean-ass whips at," JP announced with too much excitement in his voice. "Dee said you would have everything hid under floorboards like your big brother used to. We snatched up $750,000 under your baby mama's kitchen floor. I guess your ass is predictable too!"

Orlando's eyes got teary but not one tear fell from his eyelids. "So y'all in the business of hurting innocent women and kids now, Dee? Are you trying to tell me I need to make arrangements to lay my family to rest?"

My mouth still wouldn't move.

"That ain't our MO, but taping and tying up your bitch and them crying-ass kids while we cashed out on your bitch ass is!" JP responded.

"Okay, I hear you. So what's this, Demarcus? We calling the shit even now? An eye for an eye type shit?"

Orlando fell silent for a second. Then, a mischievous grin appeared on his face. "You can't talk, nigga? Wait a minute. I almost forgot! As long as you're living comfortable with all of my brother's shit, you'll always be a step ahead me, huh? I guess them long nights of sucking Gutta's kidney-failing dick paid off!"

"Keep Gutta out of this! You don't have the right to speak his name after not showing up to lay him to rest."

My mouth was open, and Orlando had gotten exactly what he wanted. He wanted to see if I still made moves with my feelings involved. And, for a split second, I did get caught up in my thoughts of how Gutta would feel about me killing his baby brother; and then my phone rang. It was my pops calling. I could tell by the ringtone. I didn't answer it, but I was glad he called. It reminded me of the first lesson he'd taught as Lord King, and that was to show no love.

When Orlando turned his back to me to talk to his boy Tay, he was overly confident that his life wasn't in danger, so I had to show him differently. My bullet went through the back of Orlando's head without warning. His boy Tay was able to pull out his gun and get two shots off. Both bullets hit JP in his chest right before Killa emptied his clip into him. When the movement stopped, I watched Killa close JP's eyes as he took his final breath among the living.

I walked away without suffering a scratch, but my stomach was fucked up. I got hit with the urge to throw up first, and then I needed to take a shit. No one who made the trip with me knew that I was in the bathroom going through it, so I couldn't understand why my pops was still blowing up my phone.

"You sure you're straight, Dee?"

Lord King had asked this same question at least one hundred times. I was fifteen minutes outside of Memphis now and had heard the same question since I'd left the truck stop. He was starting to piss me off.

"I'm good, Pops. Damn!"

"What about Killa?"

Killa, on the other hand, was fucked up. He'd spent the first hour of our ride back to Memphis crying his eyes out. I hadn't known that he and JP were day ones until we met up with Rico and Spank at the truck stop outside of Nashville. They had also suffered a casualty at Orlando's gas station. The young white boy Orlando had working there named James had caught one of my pops's goons slipping and stabbed him from his Adam's apple to his chops with a crowbar before Rico turned his white ass into Swiss cheese. Before Rico could try to get the cat some help, he took his gun to his temple to stop the pain.

Through tears and snot, Killa told us that he and JP had grown up together in side-by-side houses. Their mothers had been best friends before either one of them was born. I had never seen a man bawl out and cry the way Killa had, and I could tell that nobody else with us had either. The sympathy had turn into annoyance, and Killa had the group irritated. Because all the cars that made the trip from Memphis to Nashville were full, I put Killa's crying ass in the car with me, just in case someone said the wrong thing and set him off. Those stages of grief are real, and being in jail had taught me that the first three are the worst. Killa had already completed the denial stage when he refused to put the dead corpse down; anger was next up. Although I didn't give a fuck about the nigga, I couldn't let his anger cause one of the cats with us to kill him. I knew I could handle the crying while I was driving, but then Killa took the shit to a whole different level.

"JP! I gotcha, my nigga! I heard you loud and clear. I'm going to make that shit happen tonight. We waited long enough! Do you hear me? 'Cause I couldn't hear you. Speak a little louder!" Killa said, while having a full conversation with his deceased best friend.

After hearing the one-sided conversation for over an hour, I learned to tune him out. "Killa has had better days," was the nicest way I could answer my pops's question.

"Who's that, Dee? Is it Lord King? Tell him I need to talk to him about throwing JP's mom and baby mama some cash to ship his body home for his funeral and for his kids," Killa said, trying to take the phone from me.

Lord King had heard him. "What the fuck does he think this shit is, a Fortune 500 company? I don't pay for injuries on the job, and I don't offer life insurance policies. It was JP's job to make sure his family was straight if he got jammed. And I don't give a fuck what he says, Demarcus. I still think him and JP cleaned out that safe in your kitchen. They were the last niggas with Omar. I'm sure they—"

"I told you not to say Omar's name!" I yelled into the phone, cutting him off.

"Omar? What the fuck does big O have to do with JP's family getting what y'all owe them, Dee? I know Lord King ain't trying to pin that safe shit on us again," Killa said.

"Naw," I said, while Lord King screamed, "Hell, yeah! I am!" in my earpiece.

"Pops, the food and goodies are in the car with me. I'm going to drop the food off at our family houses, and then I'll bring you the goodies." I was trying hard to defuse the situation by quickly changing the subject.

"Come get me first. I'm feeding the family with you today. Plus, I want to know how you're feeling about all this face to face. I'm proud of you, Dee."

My pops never allowed for the dog food or vast amounts of money to be at the same place as him at the same time. For him to want to ride with me to stock up the stash houses with the dog food was a rare occasion, and I didn't want to share it with Killa and the shit he was going through.

"Where do you want me to take you?" I asked as I ended the call with Lord King.

"Shit. I'm riding with you. Tonight is the night. Ain't that right, JP?"

I wasn't going to waste time trying to figure out what his crazy ass was talking about. I made him jump in the back seat when we pulled up at Lord King's house. We waited close to five minutes before he came walking out, smiling.

"What took you so long, old man?"

"I missed your television commercial, so I had to wait for them to show it again."

"Which commercial was it?" I laughed. "Dee's Communications or the barbershop?"

Lord King cleared his voice in preparation to mock mine as he took his seat to the right of me. "'You don't always get a second chance but, then again, look at me. Do you want a new smartphone but can't afford it? Then, come into any of our three Memphis locations and leave your credit score and deposit at home. At Dee's Communications, we believe in giving second chances! *Hablamos Español.*'" He shook his head and smiled at me. "My boy, the business-man. It cracks me up every time I see you on TV, looking like an ambulance chaser in your suit and tie. You know that, boy?"

"What's up, Lord King?" Killa interrupted, changing my pops's mood.

"How are you, son?"

"Are you trying to be funny, LK? How in the fuck do you think I'm doing? I just lost my goon!"

"I didn't mean it like—"

"Then how did you mean it, nigga?"

Lord King looked at Killa and then back at me before asking, "Dee, y'all not carrying in the car, is you? I'd hate for us to get pulled over and give them pigs a reason to search us."

"No, I got Orlando with my piece. Rico is on waste management this run. He has it."

"What about you, Killa?"

"What about me, King?" he spat back.

"It's Lord King, and watch your tone, nigga. Don't forget who's writing your checks, unless you already got some bread stashed somewhere that you already took from me." Lord King took off his seat belt and took his gun out of the holster on his waist. "Here you go, Dee. I'm going to sit back there with Killa," he said, giving me his gun.

"What are you coming back here for? Stay up there." The shakiness of Killa's voice revealed his nervousness.

"We gotta discuss money for JP's family but, before that, I got a question for you."

Lord King was now in the back seat, and I was headed back to the interstate. My pops owned a huge house in Raleigh, located on the outskirts of Memphis. It was in the cut, off Austin Peay Highway, where there was a lot of farmland around him. We had a twenty-minute drive on the interstate before reaching the first stash house, and I hoped both passengers could make it that long without going off on each other.

"What happened to all that money that was in the safe? Are you sure you didn't pressure the combination out of"—Lord King looked up at the rearview mirror, when he felt my eyes on him, and he corrected his next words—"out of ol' boy before y'all disposed of him?"

"Man. How many fucking times do I have to tell your ass no? And, even if we tried to, do you think he would've given it to us, knowing he was about to die?" Killa asked, but this was the first time his answer didn't sound sincere.

"Torture is a muthafucka, Killa, and that's a specialty of yours, isn't it? Where did you say y'all dumped Omar's body again?"

Thank God I'd turned my head to hear his answer, or the bullet he shot at me would have gone through my head and not the windshield. Two more shots went off, but I couldn't tell if either one of them had been hit. They were wrestling, and one of them had opened the back door. We were on a one-way bridge with cars tailgating behind us. If I had hit the brakes, we would have all died. I couldn't pull over until I passed over the water. I sped up to put distance between us and the car behind us. When I could hit the brakes, both bodies went flying out. The car behind us wasn't prepared for what had been thrown at it, and one of my two passengers became road kill.

I jumped out as fast as I could, and in the road were two nonmoving bodies. My pops had suffered the gunshots, and Killa was now some uncouth person's meal. The guy driving the red pickup truck made it to my pops first and screamed, "He's alive! Get help!" but I couldn't turn back to my car to get my phone. I ran straight to my dad.

"Pops!" I yelled as blood poured from his stomach.

"Take me to the hospital!" was all he could say before blood trickled out of his mouth.

With help from the motorist, we got him into my back seat, and I hit 120 all the way to the ambulance entrance at Methodist Regional North Hospital.

I screamed for help, but there wasn't a need to because the ER staff had him on the gurney and in the hospital before I could get out the driver's seat.

"You're going to make it, Pops! You're a fighter!" I said, looking into his half-closed eyes.

He was trying to say something back to me, but the blood coming out of his mouth prevented me from making out his words. The doctors were giving the nurses orders as they rushed him to an elevator. I grabbed my pops's hand and held on tight.

"You're going to make it. I promise!"

"I'm sorry, sir. This is as far as you can go," one of the doctors said, but I didn't give a fuck about what he was talking about.

"This is my dad. I'm staying with him. You can kiss my ass if you think I'm not!"

I hadn't noticed security was walking down the hallway with us until he tapped me on the shoulder.

"Sir, you can't go beyond this point. Wait in the family room, and the nurses will tell you when you can see your—"

I hit the white boy in his mouth before he could finish talking, and then I hit the floor. Two other officers tackled me and pinned me down.

"Get the fuck off of me. Pops!" I yelled as the elevator doors closed and the gurney disappeared.

I sat in the security office with my hands in cuffs in front of me for fifteen minutes before they let me make a call. I gave Rico a quick run-down of what happened, and he said that he would come get the car. I had forgotten it was loaded with drugs and money because I was so caught up in all the chaos. From the security office, I could see the front desk and two plain-clothes officers with badges being directed my way.

"Hi, I'm Detective Ryu, and this is my partner, Detective Rawlings. We're from the homicide unit; and you are?" the Asian detective asked while extending his hand.

"That's Dee of Dee's Communications. You don't recognize him from the commercials and billboards all over the city?" his black partner asked as he smiled from ear to ear, looking at me like I was a celebrity.

"No, I didn't," Detective Ryu said, writing something on his tablet after realizing I wasn't in the mood for shaking hands. "Dee, is that short for something? And what's your last name?"

Before I could answer, a nurse came running into the room. "Sir, when you came in, you said that Mr. Willis is your father, right?"

"Yes!" I answered, sitting up in my seat.

"Can you uncuff him? His father is in need of a blood transfusion, stat!" the young Middle Eastern nurse said to the detectives and secu-rity guard.

"We need to ask Dee here some questions about the events that took place tonight," Detective Rawlings said while stopping the security guard from releasing me.

"That will have to wait!" the nurse snapped back.

The detectives looked from one to the other, and then Detective Ryu gave an approving nod, indicating that it was all right for the guard to release me. The nurse had me in the lab and strapped down to machines in a matter of minutes. Once they had gotten all the blood they could take from me, I was moved upstairs to the OR's waiting area. My ass barely met the seat when the detectives entered the room. They'd brought some coffee for me.

"Here you go. I didn't know if you wanted cream and sugar, so I brought you both. One with and one without," Detective Rawlings said, handing me both cups.

I knew the questions were about to roll, but instead they both took seats next to me and focused on the Memphis Grizzlies game on the TV. We sat there for an hour watching nurses come in and out to report updates on patients' conditions to their waiting families, but none ever came to me, which I thought was a good sign. On movies, doctors always come out to tell waiting family members when the patient doesn't make it. That meant my pops was back there fighting.

When my commercial came on, I couldn't help but think about what my pops had said to me. He was proud of me, and he couldn't leave without seeing me, his son, on TV. The detectives were whispering the entire time the commercial was on, and then Detective Ryu stood.

"I'm going to go get a status update on your father. If he's in stable condition, we'll need for you to come down to the station and answer a few questions for us, Mr. Elder."

He didn't give me the opportunity to respond. I guessed he had done his homework on me while I was giving blood because he knew my name. Detective Rawlings made an attempt at chitchatting but, after fifteen minutes of waiting for his partner to return, he decided to go see what was going on. They were crazy to think I'd just sit there waiting for them to return, so I went on my own little investigation. I was sure my pops was out of surgery, so I went to the nurses' station on the recovery side, but they said they didn't have him there. I decided to go back to the lab, so the phlebotomist could point me in the right direction, but they had changed shifts, and I didn't recognize any of the faces.

"Sir, are you lost?" came a voice from behind me. It was the Middle Eastern nurse who had taken me for the blood draw.

"Yes, I'm trying to get an update on my dad," I said with a smile.

"Oh, okay, have a nice night," she said, unbothered, passing me.

"Wait. Excuse me. Can you tell me who I should be asking or where to go?"

"No, I can't. I'm off!"

"I'm sorry?"

"It's okay. You didn't know," she said, turning the corner.

I walked faster to catch up. "I think you must have misunderstood me. All I need is for you to tell me where to go," I said to the back of her head.

"I'm not at liberty to give you information on our patients, sir!" she said, loudly causing the doctors and nurses who were walking down the hallway to pay more attention to us.

"Bitch, I didn't ask you for his status. I'm asking where to get it from!"

"Security!" Her yell caused the other medical personnel to call for security as well.

"Why are you fucking calling security?"

"Because you're a danger to this hospital!"

Security came running down the hallway with the detectives jogging alongside them.

"Ay, man, I'm just trying to get an update on my pops. I wasn't a threat when this ho wanted my blood!" I said to the detectives.

"You lied and said you were the patient's son. That's why I was nice to you!" she spat back.

"I am!"

"No, you're not! Your DNA wasn't a match! The test came back one hundred percent positive that you are not his son. If we wouldn't have wasted all that time with you, that man might have lived!"

"What do you mean, 'might have lived'?"

Detective Rawlings stepped up with handcuffs in his hands. "Demarcus Elder, you're under arrest for assaulting an off-duty officer, and you are the primary suspect in the murder of Mr. Keith Willis, who is better known by our narcotics unit as Lord King. You have the right . . ."

I couldn't hear my Miranda rights; everything had cut off. Not only was Lord King dead, the nigga wasn't even my father.

Chapter 3

Omar

"Symphony!"

Where in the fuck was this bitch at now? Our apartment looked like we had been hit by Hurricane Katrina and turned into the Superdome offering housing. Her homegirl Taylor had gotten evicted, and she and her four bad-ass kids had moved in with us. This bitch didn't offer us any rent money; she didn't clean for shit, and thank God she didn't offer to cook. She and her kids looked like they were suffering from malnutrition, and their cavity-filled mouths proved candy was the only full meal they were getting. I told Symphony to holler at her friend about cleaning up after herself, but she didn't. Symphony didn't want her best friend to feel unwelcome. She was afraid that if she got offended, she might move into a shelter with her kids like she had started to. Symphony wouldn't man up to her best friend; instead, she'd become the maid.

She made sure to cook and clean before and after work; but, since Symphony had gotten fired from her interpreter job at the courthouse, neither one of these bitches was cleaning shit.

I was tired of coming in every day to filth. When we moved into this apartment two years ago, we didn't have an ant, let alone a roach; but, when Taylor moved in three months ago, those nasty motherfuckas moved in with her. We had roaches in the kitchen and, once in a while, I'd killed a couple in the bathroom.

I didn't mind my woman staying at home until she found the job she wanted as long as the spot was clean, dinner was cooked whenever I walked in, and she kept them legs spread from east to west, but that was too much for a nigga to ask for nowadays. When I realized she wasn't doing her job as my woman, I started slacking on my duties as her man.

"Taylor, where's Symphony?"

Taylor was sitting on the couch, braiding the hair of one of her daughters, with a blunt in her mouth. "In her room. Damn!" she said, rolling her eyes at me.

"Damn? What the fuck you mean, damn?"

"You heard me, nigga. Do I look like your bitch's keeper?"

Taylor and her fucked-up attitude were getting old, and I wished that I wouldn't have stuck my dick in her. The first weekend she moved in here, her mother had all her kids, and Symphony and I decided to get her ass drunk and high to get her mind off her problems. I didn't know it at the time, but those hoes were setting me up from the jump. I walked back into the room from using the bathroom, and Symphony's naked ass was in the air with her head moving on overtime between Taylor's thighs.

I didn't know my baby got down with the same sex. She had never mentioned it, and she'd never asked me about having a threesome. I didn't know how to feel about watching my woman kill a cat with her tongue, but my dick said it was all good. I watched for a second and then slid inside of Symphony from the back. I was hitting it with both of my hands planted on each side of her hips, and then the shit got real.

Symphony moved one of my hands from her hips and placed it on Taylor's hard nipple. Taylor didn't have any meat on her body, but them C-cups were pretty, and that ass was fat. At my touch, that bitch purred like a feline in need of some dick. About fifty strokes later, Symphony had pulled me out of her and started sucking on my meat. It was the best head Symphony had ever given me. The head was so good I had to tilt my head back and keep my eyes on heaven, so I wouldn't blast my unwanted kids down her throat. Then, I felt Taylor's paper-thin lips wrap around my sack. Before the night was over, I had them both calling me daddy. We even slept together, all in one bed, with me lying in between them. I gave them both a good-morning ride on my early morning steel. I tongue kissed them both when we were done, and then they kissed each other.

The days that followed were cool. We all knew what had gone down, but no one had switched up. The house was functioning like the threesome never happened. It wasn't until I came home to grab my cell phone charger that the shit went sour. Symphony was at work, and Taylor wanted a one-on-one, no-holds-barred fuck session with me. The pussy was good, and her head was off the chain, so I was with it. The way I saw it was that Symphony had given me the thumbs-up to hit that every now and then. Besides, I was sure they were getting down when I wasn't home. I was stroking that cat, and then Taylor started saying all the wrong shit.

"I want this to be my dick only, daddy. Fuck Symphony's fat, sloppy ass!"

"Is that right?" I said with Taylor going up and down on my lap.

"Hell yeah! That bitch don't deserve this or you."

"Flag on the play!" I said, tossing her ass off my dick.

The mistake on my part was that I wasn't wearing a rubber and, knowing her background, she should have been riding my meat through Saran Wrap. Her mistake was thinking she could bust a snake move on my woman and that I wouldn't do or say nothing about it.

"What's wrong?" she said, staring at the lock on the door as if the only reason I'd stopped was because Symphony was home.

"Ain't shit wrong," I said, wiping off my steel with one of her kids' baby wipes and putting my clothes back on.

"Why you stop then?" she whined.

"Because I don't do raggedy pussy and you're trifling as fuck. My baby let you stay here without breaking bread, and you're ready to put her out and steal her man."

"Nigga, please! I was just talking. I don't want you. I was just saying what I thought you wanted to hear."

I looked her in her eyes, and I could see the lies swirling around her retinas. "Cool!" I said, grabbing my jacket and walking out the door.

After that, we beefed and argued about everything. I should have told Symphony about it, but I thought I handled it in the right way.

"Don't forget you're a guest in my house, Taylor!"

"I won't forget, just like you won't forget what I taste like!" she said, covering up her daughter's ears.

"Garbage!" I said as Symphony entered the room.

"Why do you come in screaming my name every damn day, Omar?" Symphony walked in with a blunt in her left hand and the remote in the other.

"Because, every time I come in from work, I come into this shit!" I said, pointing at pizza boxes on the floor, dirty laundry covering the washing machine and dryer, and the shake from weed next to blunt guts on the coffee table.

"Ugh!" she moaned and walked back to our room as I followed.

"Why does it have to be like this, Symphony? You know what? Never mind. I need you to pay the cable bill this month. My check is going to be short again. We have a lot of vacant apartments in the projects, so they haven't needed us to do any janitorial work."

I had the money for the bill, but fuck that. Symphony was getting unemployment, and Taylor got cash aid from the government and child support under the table from one of her baby daddies, and she sold her food stamps every month. I wasn't going to be the only one shoveling out cash for bills.

"Janitorial work?" Symphony said, exhaling smoke from her blunt. "I thought you were a maintenance man."

I had fucked up, but she'd never know it. "I am! That's basically the same thing."

"No, it's not. One fixes shit, and the other cleans shit. Which do you do?"

"I clean the shit I need to fix. Now get out of my face!" I said, pushing her back because she'd walked up on me.

"Lie after lie! Three years later, and you're still full of lies. You think I don't know you by now, Omar?" She pushed my forehead with the four fingers of her right hand.

"Symphony, step the fuck back! And what is that supposed to mean? You think I don't know you?"

Symphony kicked off her house slippers, decreasing her height, but she was still an inch or two taller than me. I had never dated a woman who was taller than me or who weighed more than me, but I couldn't let Symphony pass me by. She was beautiful and looked younger than her thirty-six years. I was thirty, so our age difference was never a problem. Symphony's sexy ass was the perfect combination of Hawaiian and black. Although she was L'Amir's biological sister, the only thing she'd inherited from their father was his height and voice. Their father had been in the military and, after just one look at the Pacific Islands beauty Symphony called Mom, Sergeant Millbrooks had to have her. That was the exact same way I felt about his daughter. Her pie face with those slits for eyes and succulent lips had gotten me before I was able to hear her voice. I didn't give a damn about the 210 pounds she was carrying as long as she covered me in them.

"You don't know me if you think I'm going to sit back and let a punk like you keep playing me. You think I don't know what you work on in them projects?"

Symphony was within my arms' reach, and anger was written in bold all over her face. I didn't care what she was getting ready to accuse me of as long as she didn't know about the dog food I was pushing. I'd take the bogus accusations.

"You're fixing women, or should I say broke-down, government-assistance-getting hoes," she said with a quick push to my chest, "and I'm done crying about it and stressing over you! I'm singing tonight for amateur night at the Blues House, and I pray one of those sexy brothers in there with a good job and heavy pockets wants to take me home with them because I'm going. And, if they want me to suck and fuck them, I will!"

"Bitch, please. Get somebody fucked up if you want to. You know who that thang and that mouth belong to. Don't even play with me like that. I'm not one of your bitch-ass exes who lets you do whatever you want. That's why those weak-ass niggas don't have you now." I took some of the bass out of my voice at my realization that the bitch had struck a nerve. "Come here, baby, and kiss me before I end up choking your ass out!"

She pushed me off her a few more times and then gave in. I hit it until I fell asleep. I woke up to her brother calling my cell. Her ass was gone.

"What's up?" I said into the phone while checking the time on it. It was 11:45 at night. I didn't know what time Symphony had left, but I knew she had better be on her way back.

"He wants to meet you!"

"Who?"

"Who? So you think you're an owl now? Nigga, wake up. You know who, youngster!" L'Amir was amped on the other end of the phone. "Climb out of my sister, and let's get this money. I'll be there in fifteen!"

L'Amir hung up before I could tell him the disappearing act his sister had pulled on me with that bitch Taylor. They'd gone out and left me with the kids, but I was no babysitter. Her oldest son was nine years old. He'd have to fend for his siblings until his mama brought her freaky ass back home. I'd be damned if I let babysitting make me miss out on this.

I showered and put on my clothes quick. I would normally wear my Timbs because of the two inches of snow on the ground but, that night, there wasn't shit on the ground, and I had to impress, so I threw on my Polos. I put the hood of my bubble jacket over my head and walked outside the apartment door as L'Amir pulled up.

"Don't fuck with me, L. Franco really wants to meet me?"

L'Amir hit his blunt one more time, then passed it to me. "Hit the blunt and calm your excited ass down some. Hell, yeah! He wants to meets you. He heard how you have us in the projects looking like real maintenance men while we're pushing his work. How did you get us the uniforms anyways?"

I couldn't tell L'Amir I was fucking the owner's daughter no matter how close we were. Symphony was still his baby sister. I was sure he knew I hit different shit from time to time, but to come out and just say it was crossing the line. "I'm that nigga. You know that!"

"Whatever, but listen closely. Franco wants you to do some transporting for him, but getting the job isn't going to be that easy. He's going to test you. If you pass, like I know you will, you're plugged in for life."

"And if I don't?" I asked, trying not to sound worried.

"That isn't an option with Franco. You've got to pass, like you need to pass me back my blunt. You know, one day, I'm going to kick your ass for always fucking with me."

"Shut your old ass up and drive this bitch."

These Detroit cats lived by a different set of rules than we did in Memphis, and loyalty was the first rule on their list. You couldn't be trusted in Detroit until you showed how loyal you could be. It wasn't always like that in Memphis. In Memphis, we'd go hard on a new face in our city until we got a feel for the person and then end up fucking with them until they gave us a reason not to. We're feeling-based people, and if we felt like something about you wasn't right we'd cut you off. These thought-based motherfuckas up here liked to play mind games and come up with little fucked-up tests to put you through before fucking with you, and if you failed the test or decided the shit wasn't worth your time they didn't believe in letting niggas walk away with no hard feelings. They'd kill you for having a change of heart. Like in a game of spades, if you reneged on a move you'd made, then you would have violated the rules of the game. And there'd be consequences to pay. I respected their rules. Every city has its own set and, whether I liked them or not, I had to live by them to survive, or at the very least pretend to. There wasn't a loyal bone in my body besides the ones supporting my weight. I was self-paid and self-made, so all my loyalty was to me. But I knew I could play the loyal worker role for Franco, just like I had done all those years for Lord King.

We pulled up at the Motown Museum, better known as Hitsville. I thought it was an odd place to meet in the middle of the night, but L'Amir had said, "Franco is the king of pulling odd moves. He has a real fucked-up past. If we're meeting at Motown, there's a reason for it. From the time we pull up, you're being tested. I hope your country ass knows a few old-school hits."

"What the fuck does knowing old-school hits have to do with transporting weight?"

"Fuck if I know, but the shit makes sense to Franco."

L'Amir was born and raised in Oceanside, California, and so was his army brat little sister, Symphony. The money he was making moving dog food from the West Coast to Detroit was what had made him pack up and move here. He'd moved Symphony here because of her dreams of becoming a singer. She had tried her luck in California but she was too soulful and big to get the proper notice. She was against the relocation because she knew it was going to be funded by drug money, but L'Amir had lied and said he'd retired from the fast money and was living off the profit he'd made from it, and the sweat from working nine to five on the assembly line for one of America's top three automobile manufacturers. L'Amir had only lived in Detroit for the past five years, and all he really knew was Hollywood; but not me. Detroit wasn't the only city famous for its musical history.

To my surprise, Franco was black, and he looked more like the Doggy Cartel's muscle than its drug lord. We were the same height, but he had me beat by age and about twenty pounds.

He had a potato-colored skin tone and what looked like a bald head under his skull cap. His beady dark brown eyes could scare fear into anyone, but it was his Haitian accent that made me feel uneasy.

"Omar, it is nice to finally meet you," he said, bowing at me instead of shaking my hand. "Have you been inside the museum here, yet? L'Amir said you've only been here a few years. Is this true?"

"The pleasure is all mines. I haven't made it inside of there yet. Actually, this is my first time seeing the outside of it in the three years I've lived here."

He leaked a smirk and withdrew it before it turned into a full smile. Then, he continued, "You have to go inside one day. It's a very historical place. Doesn't Memphis have something similar to it?"

"Shit! We have a few music-based museums, but the one that's similar to Hitsville is called the Stax Museum. It's dedicated to soul music. I've been in that bitch plenty of times."

I maintained eye contact with him throughout his silence. Another car pulled up, and then a van that looked like it belonged to a utility company. There was a familiar logo on the side of it, but I couldn't make it out before the van pulled over and parked. Once we were met by the newcomers, Franco started back with the small talk.

"Soul music. What would we do without it . . . and a bottle of brown liquor?" He laughed at his own joke. "The Temptations was one of my favorites that came out of here. They were the first soul singers I heard when my family moved here from Haiti in the early sixties. When I go inside Studio A, I close my eyes to try to hear their voices. I take it you know who they are. Which member is your favorite?"

That was an easy question. Hands down, I was a David Ruffin fan, but something triggered off in my head that said, *don't say David.* "I'd have to say Blue."

"Why Blue? There were more famous singers in the group than Melvin Franklin."

"It's not about the fame, Franco. That dude was loyal to the group and, most importantly, he was loyal to the group's leader, Otis. You can have Paul's, Eddie's, and David's award-winning voices, but I'll take the bass and the loyalty first any day."

Franco finally let his smile out and began talking in what sounded like French to one of the guys who came with him. Then, he turned to me and said, "Again, it was a pleasure meeting you, Omar. I would have chosen Otis because he was not only the leader, but he's the only one who's still alive."

He walked to his car and sat in the back seat. I was handed two sealed envelopes that had dates to open them on the front. L'Amir pulled off before I made it to his car, but I shortly realized why. The van that pulled up had the same logo as the uniforms I had gotten Stacey to order for us from her dad's company. The keys were in the ignition waiting for me.

The meeting had gone well, if you considered that a meeting. I had passed my test. After working for a ghost for three years who went by the name Franco, I had finally met him and was plugged all the way in. The celebrating L'Amir and I did that night lasted longer than I had expected but not long enough for me to miss seeing what Symphony had on. When I walked in at five in the morning, she had just taken off her trench coat and snow boots. She had on a black top that looked like a bra with a lot of sparkling shit on it and some little-ass blue jean shorts that showed the cupcakes that made up her ass.

"What in the fuck do you have on?" I roared at her.

"Clothes!"

"That's not clothes! You went out of here naked with all my legs, ass, and titties out!"

She laughed. "And? Madonna does it all the damn time."

"I'm not fucking Madonna. I'm fucking you. Don't you ever let me catch you outside in that again. You hear me?"

"I won't let you catch me again!" she snapped as she put the six-inch stripper heels I'd brought her to wear for me when we role-played back in their box.

"Hell naw! You wore my heels, too?"

"Last time I checked, Omar, they were my heels. You brought them for me to wear, unless you're wearing them too!"

There was something new in her voice that I didn't like. She was too confident and ready to fight. Symphony had always been a firecracker, but I had tamed those mini-explosions she used to have. She continued to stick to her guns about what she believed in, but she'd never let herself disrespect me. Tonight, however, was different. History had taught me I was in a losing battle when it came to arguing with her, so I decided to smooth it over and give her a pass this time.

"Put them heels back on for me and show daddy your performance. You haven't sung for me since my birthday last year."

"I'm not in the mood to sing for you!"

"You sang for a group of thirsty-ass niggas, so you can put yourself in the mood to sing for your man."

"I'm tired. Plus, they paid me. Remember, you want me to pay the cable this month," she said with a nasty attitude.

I dug in my pocket and pulled out a hundred dollar bill and handed it to her. "There goes the cable bill money. Now sing for daddy."

She took the money from me and put it in her purse. I couldn't see that well because her purse was on the dresser on the other side of the room, but it looked like she had a wad of money already in it. "Like I said, I'm not in the mood."

I tried all my usual tricks, but nothing seemed to work. She got in bed wearing her pajamas with the feet attached to them. I had banned her from wearing that jumpsuit to bed, unless she was on her period or battling a yeast infection. That onesie meant "don't touch me," and I vowed to burn that bitch if I ever caught it in the dirty laundry hamper. I didn't know what Symphony thought she had going on, but I knew one thing: I'd do whatever I had to do to make her fall back in love with me, and I'd bet money she'd stay that way this time!

Chapter 4

Demarcus

It was hard to believe that I was sitting back in jail, but I knew once Rico posted my bail I'd be free. I wasn't on probation, and the off-duty officer I'd hit didn't press charges. My lawyer said if the DA did decide to pick up the case, I'd get off anyway with anger management or some community service. The twelve hours I'd spent on bail hold opened my eyes back to the jailhouse lifestyle that I didn't miss.

The first time I was arrested, every nigga in there, from the holding cell until I hit population, wanted to whoop my ass. I had a rape case over my head, and niggas didn't give a damn about my side of the story. This time, I was locked up for putting an off-duty police officer on his ass, and I was getting treated like family by everyone except the staff. I couldn't trip off the slick shit the correctional officers were trying to pull, like not feeding me. There were more important issues on my mind, like why Lord King lied about being my father. I thought about it while I was waiting for them to come ask their questions in the interrogation room, and there was only one thing that made sense to me. Lord King had lied so he could use me to get his life savings back from Orlando. I didn't have proof of it, but thinking back to all the moves he'd made after we got his money back, everything he did then was suspect and unusual.

Lord King had called me every ten minutes on my ride back to Memphis. His excuse was he wanted to make sure I was straight. When I told him that we had made it back and that I had product to deliver before I could bring him his money, he volunteered to ride dirty with me. The rule was to never have him and dog food in the same place at the same time. The drug task force wanted his ass bad, but every time they ran in on him at the strip club or at his houses, he was soap-and-water clean. They couldn't catch him with shit and, the way he maneuvered, they never would.

He quickly said, "Fuck that rule," once he knew I had collected everything stolen from him, times two. If Killa's crazy ass wouldn't have been in the car with us, it might have been me dead in the middle of the road.

I had to give it to Lord King—he'd played the daddy role good. He made it mandatory that we spent time together every day, even if that meant meeting up to have a meal. On nights when I was too fucked up to drive to one of my houses, I'd crash at his place. In the mornings, he'd cook me a big-ass breakfast and, most of the time, he didn't eat a thing. Like a good parent, he wanted to make sure he fed his child before himself. The nigga even went as far as cutting my hair on a regular and cleaning up my face when I grew out my facial hair for my goatee. He was the reason I invested some of the money I'd inherited from Gutta into opening the barbershop. That was Lord King's dream before the streets had employed him and, as his son, I brought it to life. Lord King would have been the third generation of barbers in his family but, although he could cut, manual labor wasn't for him.

One night, when he was in his backyard grilling us some steaks, he told me that his fondest memories had taken place at his family's barbershop. As a child, he'd watched his grandfather cut the likes of MLK, B.B. King, Jesse Jackson, Sammy Davis Jr., and other famous cats like them. Lord King said his dad could cut his ass off too, but his grandfather had one hand in the city's black politics and the other in music, so everyone knew him and wanted to sit in his chair for the bragging rights.

His grandfather had lived through the transition from slave to freeman, but it was his father's movements that interested him the most. Lord King's father was an active member in the fight to transition from nigger to Negro. Behind his father's back, Lord King's dad would hold meetings for the militant black folks in Memphis who were ready to fight. He respected Martin Luther King Jr.'s nonviolent movement, but he wanted to ensure that Memphis was ready for war if it became necessary.

Out of all the stories he'd shared with me from the past, his fondest one was when a famous white boy singer from the West Coast walked into the all-black-staff barbershop with his celebrity friends and sat in his dad's chair. Lord King said it was the first time in his life that he saw white men treat black men as their equals. The words "sir" and "boss" weren't permitted while the guy was there, and he even went so far as asking for a barbershop nickname like his father had given to all his loyal customers. It was that story that made me want to invest in what I thought was my family's history; but it was all a lie.

"Show no love, Dee, not even to me. All I demand from you as my son and business partner is respect! Love will get you fucked up. Remember that."

He'd said those words every time I thought we were bonding, and I heard him, but I hadn't listened until now. I didn't know who Lord King had enlisted to set me up, but I knew it wasn't Rico and Spank. Those were my goons, and they couldn't be bought, even though I'd be keeping a closer eye on them after this. At this point in my life, I'd learned that I couldn't trust anyone.

Rico was waiting for me in his gal's white Honda Civic when I made bail. When I got in the car, he handed me a box of chicken with seasoned fries and a biscuit, and I swallowed it all before saying a word. "Did you bring my clothes?"

"Yep, I brought your drawers, socks, shoes, and all. I'm about to stop at this dollar store, buy you some deodorant, and ask the bitch inside to let you use the bathroom to get dressed. Hurry up and take them clothes off, so we can burn them bitches," Rico said, fully reading my mind. "Oh, and here's your phone. I cut that bitch off because it was blowing up."

I turned on my phone, and I got three notifications instantly. Visual voicemail full, text messages full, and my SMS messages was full, too. *I'll check and respond to them later.* I was sure they were questions about the causalities we'd lost in Nashville, King and Killa's fatal fight, and my arrest. If it were anything other than that, Rico would have already put me up on it.

I washed under my arms, dick, and balls with a few balled-up pieces of rough paper towel and then I got dressed. Rico was talking on his phone when I walked out of the store. He ended his conversation before I opened the car door. Shit like that wouldn't be trusted anymore.

"Who was that, Rico?"

"Aw, that wasn't nothing important. Where are we headed to now?"

He'd blatantly refused to answer my question, and it wouldn't go unnoticed. I had other things planned, but that move he'd just pulled caused me to switch things up. "Drop me off at my store on Winchester."

"I thought you said we had some moves to make," he said with too much concern in his voice.

"Change of plans."

"Whatever you say, boss. I know you need a day or two to take in everything that's happened, but Lord King is dead, and you're over the city now. We have a lot of food that needs distributing and—"

"And," I interrupted him, "you're the man's right-hand man. Handle it. Don't make any moves without getting my blessing, but temporarily you're in charge with Spank backing you. This situation I'm in isn't going to be smoothed over in a day or two. Once you drop me off, if you need to speak with me about anything dealing with dog food, come by my house. I don't want that shit nowhere near any of my businesses. If you got it in the car with you, keep going. I inherited Lord King's beef with the narcotics unit, and they will be watching me like they did him."

"That isn't all you inherited from your pops. Besides the money we got in Nashville, I'm sure he left his houses, cars, and strip club to you. I wonder what else he left you."

I wanted to tell Rico that Lord King had lied about being my father, but only the police and hospital staff knew that to be true. It was time that I stopped letting my right hand know what my left hand was doing.

We shook it up when I got out the car at Dee's Communications, and I told him I'd check in with him later that night. I was dialing Teresa from the bank number before Rico was out of sight.

"Baby, come get me. I'm at the shop on Winchester; I need to get low for the night."

I was used to her saying yes and running at my beck and call. This time, she questioned me and had hesitation in her voice. "Why do you need to get low? Are those guys who killed LK looking for you too? I love you, Dee, but you're not my man, and I'm not trying to be caught up in that."

I hung up on that ho and went through my text messages quickly. I had a few numbers that weren't programmed in my phone, and one of the unstored numbers had texted me this morning saying, Good morning. Do you have time for me today, boo?

Hell, yeah. I have time for you today. Come scoop me right now, I texted back.

I hoped it was the chick from the nail shop next door to my barbershop. She had been trying to hook up with me for a while, but I had always been too busy. The next text that came through confirmed it wasn't.

Where are you? Do you want me to meet you at your house by my aunt and uncle's?

I didn't bother texting her back. That bitch Bria wasn't getting the memo that I was done playing games with her ass. I had been blowing up her phone for two years and got nothing but her voicemail. I tried going by her family's house to see her and ended up standing in front of a judge listening to the terms of the restraining order she had filed on me. Now, the ho had heard my name ringing around the city, and she was ready to pick up the phone. When I didn't respond to her text, I knew she'd be calling me next.

"What, Bria?"

"Why haven't you returned any of my calls, Demarcus? I know you've heard my messages!"

"It's a violation of my restraining order, remember?" I laughed, lighting up a cigarette I'd bought at the dollar store.

"Are you high, Dee? And don't try to be funny. You know I had that lifted a few months ago."

I didn't say anything and neither did she. I knew the order had been lifted but, after hearing the charges that she'd made against me, I washed my hands on her ass. Every thought I had of us reuniting went down the drain when she told the judge she felt I had a hand in the disappearance of her ex-fiancé, Omar.

"You still haven't said what it is that you want with me," I spoke up once the silence had become irritating.

"I called you so we could talk. I have a lot to tell you that you need to know."

"Then talk!"

"Not over the phone, Demarcus. I want us to talk face to face." She paused for a second, then said, "Like we used to."

"This is the closest you're going to get to me, so go ahead."

"Damn, Demarcus. For real? After everything we've been through, we can't sit down and talk over a meal? I refuse to hold a conversation this serious with you over the phone. This isn't a game!"

"Say no more!" I hung up and then put her number on the reject call list with all the other numbers she'd called me from.

Bria had confessed to knowing who I was from the jump on my answering machine awhile back. There wasn't a need to talk about the shit; she'd played me. I didn't know she was my cousin's bitch, but she knew I was his little cousin. The bitch grew the balls to tell me I was everything she wanted Omar to be, but she was too scared to tell me because she thought I would call it quits when I found out. She assumed Omar had told me who she was when she found the heroin in my pocket; but, with the help of her family and multiple hours of therapy after her suicide attempt, she realized that I hadn't known. It was too late for all of that now; she'd have to chalk up the entire situation as a loss. Hell, I had.

When her text message came through saying that her mysterious ex was my cousin, I didn't give a fuck. I was in love with Bria; she was my world, and if she was Omar's ho then fuck it. I was ready to live with the fact that she would be my ho too. But that was the greener version of me thinking. Life had dished out a lot of fucked-up lessons in the past few years, and my fake father had helped me get through all of them, including her.

Bria wasn't "the one" like every man waited for. She wasn't worthy to carry neither my last name nor my child. I needed a woman who could hold me down and take my wrongdoings to the grave with her. Telling the judge I had something to do with Omar going missing was more than enough proof that she wasn't my queen. Hell, her loyalty and heart seemed to still be with Omar. I had to fight that nigga in life; there was no way I would fight him for Bria's heart in death.

She didn't know the man I had become. When I'd met her, I was fresh out of jail and waiting to turn twenty-one. She cut all ties with me a few months shy of me turning twenty-five, and I was closer to finding my way. Three years and six months later, I was knocking at twenty-nine's doorstep, and I knew that the bitch wasn't worthy to breathe the air in my world. I went from renting a motel by the week to keep a roof over my head to having three different spots in my name to rest my head in. I went from selling crumbs and transporting heroin to running an enterprise of large distributors down South. I had niggas getting their hands dirty for me, so I could sit back and brand myself legitimately through all the businesses I owned. I thanked Gutta, Rico, Spank, and even Lord King's lying ass for giving me the tools to do it with.

Bria needed to bottle up all that love she claimed to still have for me and give it to someone else to sip from. If that bitch thought Omar had done her in, she didn't want a taste of the hell I could cause her. *She'd better go find the next sucker to lick on because there is no candy left on this stick. I'm labeled all natural, no sugar added.*

"Nephew."

I didn't need to turn around to know it was Uncle Leroy calling my name. "What's up, Unc?"

He was sitting on the passenger side of an old-school Grand Marquis, but when he saw me he came running my way. "Are you okay? Word around town is that you and Lord King fucked over some niggas from New Orleans, and they came to peel y'all's cap back. They said them niggas got LK and Killa, but you pulled a bitch move and took off running during the shootout. They said you left your pops and Killa to die while you saved your own ass. What type of shit is that, nephew? You're out here looking real bad."

"That's bullshit. It didn't even go down like that. That whole story is bogus as fuck. Who's going around saying that shit?"

Uncle Leroy was fidgeting and couldn't stay still if he were paid to. That monkey was on his back bad, and I could tell he needed a fix. "Shit, I heard it from . . ." He started snapping his fingers above his head like it would help jog his memory. "Well, to keep it real with you, since you're my favorite nephew, I didn't hear the shit from nobody." He broke out in laughter. "That's the story I've been telling folks when they asked me what happened, but if you give me three dollars right now, I won't tell it to anybody else." He held up the peace sign and then said, "Scout's honor."

"You ain't no scout, Unc. You're a big-time pimp." I had to laugh at my own attempt to gas him up.

"Damn right. I'm a big-time pimp, the biggest pimp Memphis has ever seen. You know they've been talking about putting me in history books and the museums here, right? But don't try to change the subject. I still need them three dollars to keep my mouth closed and an extra five dollars to put in that ho's gas tank for bringing me to find you."

He pointed at the car, but I couldn't see who the driver was. She didn't look like one of the junkies Unc was usually with, but that didn't mean shit. I had lawyers and city bus drivers for customers. Some folks just know how to function on drugs, but it doesn't last long. I gave him twenty dollars.

"You think you can get that ho to drop me off, Unc?"

"Does a pussy have lips? Hell yeah, nephew. Let me go tell her what she about to do next. These hoes need guidance."

I watched Unc walk to the driver's side window and start talking. I couldn't hear their conversation, but I heard the car crank up, and the driver smashed out of the parking lot, leaving Unc there to talk shit to her taillights.

"Damn, Unc. What happened?" I asked, laughing at the names he was calling the girl.

"I don't know. I told the bitch who you were, and she got star struck, I guess. She said, 'Dee from the commercial?' and when I said yes, the bitch smashed off."

"You let one of your hoes drive off on you, Unc? I thought you said you were a pimp."

"Watch your mouth, nephew. You know not to question the strength of my pimp hand, and she wasn't one of my hoes. She's my bottom bitch's daughter."

"Aww, okay. That's your step-daughter," I joked.

Unc knuckled up, and we began play fighting in the parking lot. I had him in a choke hold, and he was about to tap out when a familiar beige Impala pulled up.

"Mr. Elder, we need to bring you in for some more questioning," Detective Ryu said, jumping out the passenger's side.

"Which Mr. Elder are you talking to, Chinese man?" Uncle Leroy said in what he thought was an Asian accent.

"He knows who I'm talking to."

"What do y'all want to question me about now? I told you what happened with Lord King already," I snapped.

"No, I don't think that was the entire truth. We think you left a few things out. Hop in the back seat."

I stared at Unc, hoping he would say something to get me out of it, but he didn't. He looked back at me and said, "Are you about to go snitch, nephew? It's going to cost you another twenty dollars if you don't want me to tell everybody that you're a CI now." He turned his back to me with his palm out to receive the money. "Ay, Chinaman, if you're taking your CI downtown to 201 Poplar, let me get a ride down there too. I need to get to the bus station, so I can get back to Westwood before my hoes start worrying about me."

"No problem. We'll drop you off. Let me see your identification to make sure we don't need to bring you in for questioning too," Detective Rawlings said with his head out the window.

Uncle Leroy started walking backward, away from all of us. When he gave himself a decent head start, he took off running and yelled, "I just remembered I don't like pork, you pigs."

"Should we go get him and see what he's hiding?" Detective Ryu asked his partner.

"Naw, let him go. We'll catch him next time. We have bigger fish to fry right now." Rawlings turned his attention back to me. "Are you getting in by your own will or do we need to help you?"

***

They put me in the same interrogation room I had been questioned and arrested in for the rape. I had fucked up back then by answering their questions before my lawyer came. I wouldn't fuck myself twice. They tried to ask me questions before Jacob made it, but I stayed quiet.

"We went to notify Calvin's mother—sorry, you knew him as Killa—that he was dead and had committed a murder seconds before his life was taken, and do you know what his mother told us?" Rawlings asked.

"Naw, I don't have a clue."

"She told us that less than fifteen minutes before we pulled up, she was notified that her godson had been killed in Nashville. A guy named Jessie, but you would have known him by a different name. What was his other name, partner?"

"They called him JP. I think that's what she said," Ryu chimed in.

"Yes, that's it, JP. Does that ring any bells?" Rawlings asked with a smile on his face, but I didn't respond.

"So let's do the math. JP and Killa are god-brothers. JP's open case in the narcotics unit has him listed as working for Lord King, who Killa killed in the back seat of your car less than four hours after Nashville's homicide unit identified

JP's body. Partner, do you want to tell Mr. Elder here what else we found out?"

"No, partner. You can tell him," Ryu said, drinking his coffee.

"Then, let me continue. Nashville found two bodies with JP, and one of those victims had been killed by the same gun that killed Lord King; and the other body, well, we'll just say that the killer is still on the loose, but guess who the other person was?"

I stayed silent.

"Come on, Mr. Elder. Humor us with a guess."

I looked Rawlings in his eyes and didn't say shit.

"I think he knows who it was, partner," Ryu said.

"I think he does too, but let's pretend he doesn't and tell him. The other victim's name was Orlando, and Orlando had an older brother named Greg. You know Greg, Mr. Elder. We are sure you do because Greg died of . . . What was it again, partner?"

"The death record reads kidney failure, partner."

"Right," Rawlings said like he didn't already know the answer. "He died of kidney failure three years ago, and you were named the executor of his estate. Not his brother Orlando, but you. Why is that? You aren't related to anyone alive in Memphis, besides a guy named Omar, who is currently on our missing persons list, and a felon named Leroy, who I take it we just met. Why would a man work his ass off at a sheet metal company for over twenty years and leave everything to his ex-employee?"

My face told on me as shock fell on it. *How in the fuck did they find out all of this in less than twenty-four hours?* If the detectives were always this good at what they did, I would have been sentenced to life in jail before sunrise for Orlando and the other two cats I killed last year.

"Don't worry about explaining why he left everything to you, because that isn't a crime. Shit happens. What we do want to know is what is your tie to all of this? I mean, did you go to Nashville with Killa, JP, and Lord King? Who killed Orlando? Why did Killa turn on his boss? Help us to put this puzzle together, Mr. Elder. It's not like we can bring all of the other parties in, because everyone else is dead." Rawlings shut his mouth for a second but came and sat on the table inches from me.

"Everyone is dead, Mr. Elder, everyone but you. You can stay quiet until your lawyer comes, but if you do then I feel it would be our public service to help Nashville with their triple homi- cide case. You see, Nashville doesn't know what we know yet, or they would be trying to work with us to have your property searched for the murder weapon. We'd be testing your clothes and skin for gun residue and making it real hard for you to breathe air outside the jail cell until you go to court."

"But it's no secret that Memphis and Nashville don't get along," Detective Ryu said, walking up behind me and putting his hands on my shoulders. "Why should we help them put you away for life when they think we are below them? If we helped their investigation, they wouldn't give us credit for being smarter than them, so why should we help?"

"Because it's our duty as officers of the law, Ryu. We took an oath, and we have to stand by it, unless . . ."

"Unless what, partner?"

"Unless Mr. Elder here helps us and the narcotics unit close our cases with all that information he has locked in his head. I might forget to mention our findings to Nashville. I mean, Nashville doesn't even have the murder weapon. Without help from us, this case has a good chance of becoming another cold one."

Detective Ryu squeezed my shoulders tight before saying, "This is a no-brainer, so what do you say, Mr. Elder, are you going to help us?"

The deal sounded too good to be true. I wanted to take it, but agreeing to take it would make me seem guilty of something and put me in Nashville at the time of the triple homicide. I also didn't know what case or cases the narcotics unit was working, but I knew they had been watching Lord King. If they had been watching him, then they had been watching me, Rico, and Spank too. I wasn't a snitch, and these detectives weren't going to make me out to be one, either. Just when I had made up my mind, it was spoken for me.

"Get your hands off my client and, Mr. Elder, don't say another word. Do you have any charges to hold him on?" a tall woman with dark skin asked the detectives. Her dreadlocks were neatly tied into a low ponytail. She wasn't my lawyer, but maybe Jacob had sent her from his firm.

"We are almost certain we have motive, and before you walked in your client was making a deal with us to get himself a lower sentence," Rawlings told her.

"A lower sentence on what charge?" She looked at both detectives. "You don't have anything to charge him with. You were digging for a confession, fellas, and failed epically. Here's my card. Call us when you have some evidence. Almost doesn't count. And don't worry. My client won't be traveling or leaving the city anytime soon.

Only the guilty flee. You gentlemen have a nice day. Mr. Elder, after you."

I didn't know who this bitch was, but I was in love. She darted out of the police station like a bat on fire. She didn't say anything to me when we got in her car, so I thought I'd break the ice.

"You gave them hell back there. Thanks. They were trying to get me to—"

"Shut up! Sit your clown ass back and listen to me carefully. First and foremost, I don't discuss my cases, or anything else someone may find incriminating, in my car. There's a time and place for all of that, and my Benz isn't one of them. Secondly, I haven't decided yet if I'm taking your case, so consider this a taxi ride; and, last but most importantly, I graduated from Harvard Law first in my class and was offered positions at some of the top firms from California to New York. I know I'm the shit and I'm the best at what I do. Please don't think you can flatter me with praise. I praise myself daily."

With her last words, she turned the volume up on her CD player, and Minnie Ripperton's "Memory Lane" came blazing through the speakers with so much clarity you'd think we were watching her live. I was going to compliment her system, but I was sure the overly confident bitch complimented herself on that daily, too.

She didn't ask me where I wanted to be dropped off. She took me straight to my house on Bluebell Cove. It was the house I grew up in and the same house Omar had turned into his. I hadn't stepped foot in the house since that Saturday morning I ran in there on Omar, the same Saturday Lord King confessed to being my father. I didn't need to be in this house right now.

"Excuse me," I said, prompting her to turn her music down. "I need you to take me to my other place. I don't lay my head here."

"You will tonight," she confidently said.

"No, I won't; and if you're a taxi driver, you take the passengers to where they want to go."

She had taken the keys out of the ignition and she was out of the car before I could continue my protest. When she realized I wasn't following her, she came and opened my car door. "Get your ass out of my car now. There's a reason for everything."

I got out of her car, but I wasn't going into the house. I sat on the porch and pulled out my phone. I'd have Spank take me home.

"Put the phone away. We have work to do. Until this problem of yours goes away, you will sleep here. Staying in the house that the murder victim's brother gave you or the one you got as a gift from Memphis's biggest drug lord isn't ideal right now."

I heard her and had to agree with what she was saying, but I had to clear one thing up first. "You said we have work to do. Did you decide to take me on as a client, miss?"

She grabbed my face and forced eye contact with me. "I'll let you know after you tell me the truth and not that bullshit story you fed the detectives yesterday. I need to know everything, including what you told them when you were questioned today. Once you've done that, I'll let you know; and it's Ms. Claybrooks, but you can call me Joyce."

I unlocked the front door and stepped to the side. "Boss bitch lawyers first."

She smiled at me, then walked in. This was going to be interesting. I could feel it.

Chapter 5

Omar

Detroit, Michigan. Population: 700,000 people, and almost half of these motherfuckas knew somebody who used heroin. I guess you could say it's my kind of place since unemployment would never be an issue for me. These grimy-ass streets would always need a pharmacist, and I was the right nigga for the job. After being muscled out of Memphis by an organization of hoes and getting plugged in with the soul music–loving Haitian who had the dog food industry on lock, setting up shop in Detroit was easier than I'd thought it would be. My only issue was hiding my true career from my woman, who was losing more feelings for me every time the sun set.

I didn't want to do it but, because I loved her, I couldn't sit back and let her go. It was time to concoct my fail-proof love potion that I had only used once before, and that was with Bria's ass.

I needed Symphony to be as addicted to me as Bria had been, and dog food was the way to do it. I started it off slowly, by sprinkling some heroin dust in the blunts I rolled for her, but that wasn't enough. The small amount of the drug had only made her more open to freakier shit in the bed. She still talked shit, and her going out went from twice a week to daily. It was time to step my game up.

I had heard that a famous actress said she got addicted to cocaine because her ex used it so much it was in his semen and that he would rub it on his meat before she gave him head. I wasn't going to start shooting it up, but rubbing it on my meat was worth a try. I waited to give it a try until she came home from the blues spot she had been singing at. Taylor and her kids had gone to her mother's house to celebrate Halloween and the other upcoming holidays, so we'd have the apartment to ourselves until the New Year arrived. I was sitting on the couch, smoking a blunt, when she came in dressed as a sexy witch.

"What I tell you about going out naked?"

"This is a costume, Omar. I'm a performer, or did you forget?"

"If you have to dress like that to sing, you need to quit unless you're stripping while you're singing. If that's the case, I need to be kicking your ass."

She threw her witch's hat at me. "Fuck you! And if I was stripping, your ass wouldn't know anyways because you haven't come to none of my performances. I've been working there for three months, and I haven't seen my so-called man in there yet. You don't give a fuck about my dreams, do you, nigga? Let me hit your blunt."

"Hell naw! I don't know where your mouth has been because it sho' ain't been on me. There's another blunt rolled in the ashtray."

She snatched the heroin-laced blunt and began puffing on it and talking shit at the same time. I kept the argument going, which caused her to hit the blunt harder and inhale it longer. Her eyes were low, and her words were slower before she placed the roach of her blunt in the ashtray.

"Where has your mouth been, baby?" I asked, walking up behind her and planting small kisses around her neck.

"Move, Omar. If you really don't know where my mouth has been, stop kissing on me. I should be asking your hoeish ass where your mouth has been."

She told me to move but tilted her head to the right to give me more access to her neck. One rub on her erect nipples told me she wanted some of this dick.

"I just miss that mouth of yours, baby," I said, now tracing her lips with my finger. "Can daddy feel them lips on me?"

She turned around on the couch and put her weight on her knees. She started unbuckling my pants, and I helped her out. She took my semi-hard meat into her mouth and made the whole thing disappear like I wasn't working with nine inches. I let her do her thing for a minute or so.

"Baby, if I pour honey on my dick, will you suck my shit clean?"

Without taking my steel out of her mouth, she nodded her head. I let her suck it for a few seconds more. Then, I went into the kitchen with my pants and drawers around my ankles. I took the dog food out of my pocket and poured it into my hands and then poured the honey on top of it. I didn't like my meat sticky unless it was covered in pussy, but I had to kill the bitter taste of the heroin. Once I mixed the shit to what I thought was perfect, I rubbed it all over my dick and reentered the room.

"Here you go, baby. Come get it. But take them panties off and crawl to it." She stood up and began taking her skirt off. "No. Leave the skirt on. Just pull it up a little more. I want to see it caress that ass. Follow directions and take them panties off."

She did and crawled to me slowly. When she made it to me, I made her suck my hands clean before she put my meat back into her mouth. She was doing her thing, and I had no complaints. My meat was harder than I had ever seen it before. If Symphony had made the mistake of biting me, she would have chipped a tooth. There was spit everywhere, just like I liked it, and she was gagging with tears in her eyes but she continued to put me deeper into her mouth. I closed my eyes and, next thing I knew, I felt heat. Symphony had thrown up all over my shit, but her vomiting didn't stop. She threw up for about thirty minutes. I had used too much dog food, and she was having a first-time user's reaction.

"Are you okay, baby?"

"Yes. I tried to swallow with you down my throat, and it went down the wrong pipe. That's all. I don't have anything on my stomach but liquor."

"Are you sure?" I asked, trying to sound concerned. When she nodded her head, I jumped in the shower. From that night on, whenever I fed her this dick, I made sure to feed her ass some dog food, too.

The love potion had worked, and I had my woman back better than I had her before. She started putting me first, and going to perform was now a thing of the past. Everything was going good until L'Amir had gotten jammed up on a run we made to Milwaukee. The entire trip was fucked up. The contact decided, once we arrived, that he didn't like our prices, so we made the trip with all of that heroin for nothing. I was ready to hit the road and get back to Detroit, but L'Amir insisted we hit a club before we left.

L'Amir let his dick drive, and he left me at the club to take two bitches to a motel for a night of fun. Three hours later, he was calling me in tears, saying that they had robbed him for everything: money and the company truck we'd used to move the dog food. Before I could come up with our next move and a story for Franco, we got pulled over for speeding in the rental I got, and L'Amir was arrested for driving on a revoked license and for a parole violation. He wasn't supposed to leave the state. He had a hold on him and couldn't be bailed out, so I had to leave him. On the ride back to Detroit, my mind was filled with stories to tell Franco, but none sounded believable, so I was going to tell him the truth as soon as I got back, but it was too late.

"How was work, maintenance man, janitor, and drug dealer? It took me awhile to figure out why I was waking up in cold sweats whenever you weren't around, but Franco gave me what I needed."

"Franco was here?" I'd heard what she said, and the cat was out of the bag. There wasn't a need to try to keep my lie going.

"Yep. He came looking for you. He said my brother called him from jail saying he had been robbed and the police were holding him on a violation. He was pissed off, too. He said you hadn't picked up the phone to tell him anything. He saw me going through withdrawal and left me a little package to help me get through it. You need to get your shit and get the fuck out."

She ran up on me, but I wasn't worried about her hitting me. She had lost so much weight over the last two months that I knew a hit from me would put her down. She hit me in my mouth, and then I knocked her on her ass.

"Bitch, you thought I wouldn't hit your ass back? Run up again if you're bad."

There was a knock on the door, and Symphony was making her way back to the room, crying and yelling. I went to open the door, but Franco came in using Symphony's keys.

"Why haven't I heard from you, Omar? What happened to my product?" Franco said entirely too calmly.

"L got robbed by some bitches and then got caught up with the police."

"I know. He called me immediately, but why haven't I heard from you? You had your freedom, yet you didn't use that as an opportunity to call me. What does that say about you, Omar?"

"That I'm not a damn fool to talk business over the phone. I was going to tell you as soon as I made it back."

"But you didn't. You came home to your heroin-addicted girlfriend. Whose dog food are you feeding her? She told me she never paid for anything and she didn't know that you had been giving it to her."

"That bitch knew. She's just in denial about the shit, and I wasn't stealing shit from you. Anything I gave that ho I made sure to deduct from my pay for it."

He closed and locked the door behind him. When he turned around to face me, he had a silencer pointing at me.

"My father told me, before he was murdered by a ghost from his past, a story about some savages from Memphis he had to dispose of. He warned me never to trust anything that came out of Tennessee because they were backward people and not worthy of trust. His brother, Jean Paul, who was my uncle, had been murdered by a man and his heroin-addicted wife. It wasn't a family secret that Jean Paul went crazy before we made it to America, but he was a good businessman, and he tried to build an empire with those Memphis pieces of shit. It's seems like you and your girlfriend are trying to make me suffer that same fate."

"Y'all Haitian niggas talk too much," was all I heard before the sounds of two shots went off.

Symphony had shot Franco in his shoulder and arm, causing him to drop his gun. I picked it up and finished him off with it.

"That couple your dad killed were my parents, bitch."

I knew he was dead, but I couldn't stop filling his body with lead. It wasn't until I realized that Symphony had her gun pointed at the back of my head and mine was empty that I snapped out of it. I knew I was only a few seconds away from death because, after hearing what she'd said to Franco, I knew Symphony would shoot before talking.

"It doesn't have to be like this, Symphony."

"Yes, it does," was all I let her say before I snatched my gun from my waistband and put a bullet in between her breasts.

She fell back onto the couch like a paper airplane gliding through the air. When the blood bubbled out of her mouth, releasing her soul from her flesh, I grabbed the gun I had killed Franco with, wiped off my prints, and placed it in her free hand, making sure to point it in the direction of the bullets I had put into him. My fingerprints were all over the apartment, and there wasn't time to play pack up and clean up, so I grabbed my ID and all of my cash and started planning my escape.

I knew Franco didn't drive himself, so walking out the front door wasn't an option. I grabbed the dish sponge out of the dirty water in the kitchen sink and put it in the microwave on high. Before making my way out the fire escape, I pulled the natural gas line out of the back of the stove. If my fifth grade science teacher was as smart as he claimed to be, once the sponge dried out completely, it would catch fire, and that would be all she wrote. I was in the car and backing out when the windows of the apartment blew out. *I guess that mother-fucka was right.*

I needed to move fast and stay busy to keep my mind off Symphony. She was the first woman I had ever loved, besides Bria, and I had fucked that up, too. My love was poisonous, and everyone I'd ever loved turned sick or died: My parents, Bria, Symphony and, although I'd never admit it to anyone, my aunt Sharon too.

She gave birth to that bitch Demarcus, but that was really her only flaw. She took me in and cared for me when nobody else cared. Lord King did too, but I'd never looked at him as a father figure. From the first day he put me on as a lookout for his stash house, I wanted to knock him from his spot. But, with Aunt Sharon, she was the mother I wished my mother had been. I guess that was why I hated her so much. She was a constant reminder of what my mama was doing wrong, and when my mother died, I finally got the chance to experience what a mother's love was really like. That woman did everything for me, and when she told me she had cancer and didn't have long for this world, the hate I had learned to bury for her came back with a vengeance. She was leaving me, just like my mama had done, and there was no forgiving that. In our last conversation, I'd let her know it, too.

"Did Demarcus accept your visit?" she asked, *lying in her hospital bed with machines hooked up to her from head to toe.*

"Naw."

"Did you write him and tell him about me?"

"Naw," I said, getting angrier by the second.

"Omar, this is it for me. I'm not coming back home. I need you to let Demarcus know that I am dying and that I love him. I need you to be

my legs for me and make sure the house note gets paid, so he can always have somewhere to lay his head."

"What about my head?" I snapped. "What the fuck am I supposed to do you when you die?"

She tried to pull herself up into a sitting position, but the energy wasn't there. She pushed the button on the side of the bed, and it sat her up. "I love you, Omar, and over the years you've become my oldest son, especially since Demarcus has been gone. I need you to be the strong man you've always been and do what is right. Take all my money out of the bank like I told you to, pay the house note up for your cousin, and get you an apartment with the rest. You should have enough to pay your rent up six months and, if you don't, all that drug money you have stashed under the floorboards in your closet should be enough."

I was shocked that she knew about my stash.

"A mother knows everything. Don't look shocked." *She mustered up a weak smile.* "You've been working for Lord King for years. He's a real close friend of mine, and I told him he better take damn good care of you and never let you get caught up because of him. He kept his promise to me, so there wasn't a need to bring it to your attention. Come closer to me, Omar."

I didn't want to come closer, but her eyes were begging me to. With every step I took closer to her, I could smell the death on her, and the scent was breaking my heart. I didn't know what to do, but crying wasn't an option, so I snapped on her.

"Fuck you, Sharon. You ain't my mama. You're a fill-in and a horrible replacement. And don't try to make the shit sound like you and LK are good friends. I know he used to buy that pussy, just like the rest of Westwood. Once a ho, always a ho in my eyes."

"Omar!" she tried to yell, but it came out as an airy whisper.

"Don't 'Omar' me, bitch. This is my last time coming to this bitch, too. I just stopped by to tell you that I wasn't your messenger and that I wasn't going to tell your faggot-ass son shit. I cleaned out your banking account this morning and spent all of it on heroin. That little bitch of yours is going to be homeless, and there ain't shit you can do about it. Rest in piss, bitch."

I walked out holding on to my tears until I made it to the elevator. Once I walked inside of it, I pulled the emergency stop and hit the floor, crying. I cried until my tear ducts dried out and I promised that those would be the only tears I'd drop over her ass. She had left me just like my mama had. Fuck Sharon.

I drove forty miles from Detroit before I stopped and filled up in Monroe, Michigan. My thoughts of the past were attacking me, and being fucked up was the only thing that always made me feel better.

"911. State the nature of your emergency."

"I have information on a double homicide," I said into L'Amir's personal cell phone. It wasn't the burnout that Franco had given him. It was the one he had in his name for his family in California to reach him on.

"What is the address where the murder has taken place?"

"Listen, bitch. The murder took place in Memphis years ago, but I know who did it now. There was a husband and wife found dead and naked in the Mississippi River in 1995. They were killed by the heads of the Doggy Cartel from Detroit. The nigga who pulled the trigger was killed years ago, and his bitch-ass son was just murdered, but the Doggy Cartel is still operational and filling the streets of Detroit with heroin."

"What is your name, sir? I'd like to send a car to take this report. Your claims are very serious and—"

"You don't need to take a report. This call is recorded, and I didn't witness any of this shit.

Franco, the new leader of the cartel, confessed it to me moments before his death. You should send a squad car to Mack Avenue and Bewick Street to check out that refrigerated truck parked by the store. It will be an epic drug bust for the city."

"Sir, did you witness this Franco's murder? How do you know all of this?"

"Yep, he was killed by one of his sales in an apartment off West 7 Mile Road. I got the rest of my information from the nigga whose phone I'm using. He owns that truck I told you about and is in the infamous Doggy Cartel too." My next words came out choked up, but I was sure she understood me. "And those dead naked people from Memphis were my parents."

I took the battery out of the phone, threw it on the concrete, and smashed it into little pieces before I jumped back on Highway 75. Every fiftieth mile I passed, I threw a portion of the cell phone out the window after wiping it off. I didn't stop again until lunchtime, which meant I was five hours away from Detroit.

"What's up, beautiful? Did you miss me?"

I had snuck up on Unique as she was getting out of her car to walk into her job.

"Oh, hell naw! Where's my money at, nigga?" she screamed at me and began looking around for help.

"Money? What in the fuck are you talking about? I haven't seen your ass in three years, and you're accusing me of stealing money. Here, I'm not even trying to argue with your ass over something petty when a nigga has been missing you. How much do you claim I stole?" I said, pulling out a stack.

"You stole like three hundred out of my purse. Don't play dumb."

"I didn't steal shit, but here goes a stack. Are we good again?" I asked, handing her ten crisp hundred dollar bills. Unique held each bill to the sun, checking their authenticity like a store owner. Then, she nodded her head.

"So are you ready to go have lunch and get a little shopping in? Victoria's Secret got some shit I want to see you in."

Like the dumb bitch I thought she was, she started smiling and then said, "I can't. I have to work. Maybe this weekend, though. I'm off on Saturdays."

"Come on, baby. I know I gave you more money than you make flipping burgers in a week. I need you today."

"I'm the manager now," she said, catching an attitude like I had insulted her choice of career. "I can't just take off of work because you popped up after three years. You didn't even try to call me."

"You didn't give me your number, and I didn't know the name of the street your burger spot was on. I tried looking it up," I lied. "If you're the boss, go in and pull a boss move. I know you have an assistant manager or a shift lead you can leave in charge for the day. Please?"

She stared at me for a second, then said, "I'll be right back," and went inside. She came back out with a spaghetti-strap shirt on but she was still wearing her ugly navy blue uniform pants. After a few minutes more of spitting game at her, we were in her car, headed to Mall St. Matthews to eat at the Cheesecake Factory. I fed her and spent about $700 on her at the mall. I could tell she'd never had a nigga spend money on her because she didn't know how to get me to break more bread, and I wasn't about to teach her how to gold dig. That was her mammy's job.

"Can we go get a room and finish enjoying our night?" I begged.

"I can't. I, umm, I live with my boyfriend, and if I don't come home tonight, he'll pitch a fit."

"Fuck that nigga." I said it with too much jealousy in my voice, but that was how I felt. "I don't see him putting money in your pocket and taking you on shopping sprees. I bet he's flipping burgers too."

"He doesn't," she spat back. "He's a forklift driver."

"Am I supposed to be impressed? Call that nigga and tell him that it's over. Daddy's home to stay."

"But if I do that, I won't have anywhere to stay, and he's so childish. He'll probably tear up all the stuff I have at his place. I can't just call him up—"

I cut her off. "You'll stay with me. I'm about to get an apartment here tomorrow and fuck that shit you got at his spot. I'll replace all of it and then some. Call that nigga, baby."

"Are you serious, Omar? I don't even know your last name."

"You will," I said. "I'm going to make it yours. My last name is Brown." I didn't know where the last name Brown came from, but it was the first name to come to mind, so I let it roll off my tongue. "Call him, beautiful. I have plans for us."

She called, and they argued for a few minutes, and then I couldn't take the yelling anymore so I snatched the phone from her.

"Listen, my nigga. The shit y'all had going on, it's a wrap. Thanks for holding my lady down while I came up, but your services are no longer needed."

I hung up on him, grabbed her hand, and held it as I walked her into the first jewelry store I saw. "Pick out your ring, baby. I'm going to make this engagement official."

Everyone in the jewelry store smiled and congratulated us. With the help of an old white lady who was in the store getting her diamonds polished, Unique picked out a $1,400 ring. They boxed it up all nice and pretty, and I paid for it.

"Can I wear it now, daddy?"

"Naw, baby. We're going to do this the right way. Call your folks and invite them to dinner Friday night. I'm going to propose to you in front of them and ask them for your hand in marriage."

She screamed excitedly, pulled out her cell phone, and called her mom. She told me her mother had raised her alone and that she knew who her father was, but he didn't have a role in her life.

"That's cool and all, baby, but on our wedding day when you come walking down that aisle to me dressed like my guardian angel, I need your pops escorting you."

Unique wasn't thrilled about me forcing her to involve her father, but she agreed to my terms. And then we both agreed she could call him when the wedding date was set. We checked into the Seelbach Hilton, and I gave her the money to get us a junior suite for the week. I told her I didn't know how long it would take to get us an apartment but, as her man, I had to make sure we had a roof over our heads. I handed her a hundred dollars once we were settled in and told her to go get us a box of condoms, a bottle of Rémy, and some loud. She was mad I hadn't asked her to get it on the way to our hotel and was forcing her to go back out.

"I'm sorry, baby, but I'm in the mood to celebrate. Scratch that bottle of Rémy. I'll have the hotel bring us the most expensive bottle of champagne they got, but you still gotta go get the green and some condoms."

"What do we need condoms for if we're about to get married?"

"Because I don't want to feel that thang without one until our wedding night. Do you love me like I love you?"

She thought about it, which surprised me. I was moving fast and, up until now, she had been moving at the same pace.

"Yes, I love you, but how do you know I'm the one?"

"Baby, I knew I had to have you when you broke your ass to feed me. I was broke then, and I told myself if I ever struck it rich, I'd come back and get you. So I did."

"But how did you get rich? You're not on the run or nothing, I hope."

"Hell naw," I said while thinking of my next lie. "My family in Detroit died, and I inherited everything. I sold their houses and shit, but I still own a few stores up there."

"What kind of stores, and why aren't we moving there to manage them?"

"Baby, what's up with the thousand questions? If you don't want to marry me and live a luxurious life, say it, and I'll take my ass back to Detroit, heartbroken."

"No, daddy, I do. I'm going to go get the weed now. I love you."

"Back at you, beautiful."

I couldn't wait for her to leave to pull the dog food out of my jacket pocket. I held it in my hand and gave it my full attention. I didn't know why I felt the need to look at it, but I did. It was amazing how something that could fit in the palm of a closed hand could destroy lives. When I was done playing with it, I flushed the remainder I had in my pocket down the toilet.

"Adios, you dangerous motherfucka."

I was watching *SportsCenter* and sipping on the nasty-ass champagne the hotel had brought us when she came back. Unique sat down, broke down the weed, and rolled the blunt tighter than a virgin sitting in a tub of hot water and vinegar doing Kegel exercises.

"Look at my queen, rolling blunts for her king."

She took a few hits off the blunt before passing it to me. "That isn't all your queen is going to do for you," she said, falling to her knees.

She collapsed her head in my lap and put her mouth to work as I smoked. I grabbed the condoms off the coffee table and banged her back out like I used to do the junkies in exchange for dog food when their money was short. When I was done, I passed out next to her on the couch.

She woke me up the next morning after ordering and paying for our breakfast. "Daddy, I have to go to work, and it's my long day. I have to pull a ten-hour shift."

"No, baby, don't go." I tried to sound devastated.

"I have to. You haven't retired me yet," she said with a giggle.

"Okay, baby, but I'm retiring you soon, so start looking for a replacement. Here goes the keys to my SUV. I'm going to drop you off at work and use your car to go apartment hunting, okay, baby?"

"Okay, daddy, but we have to go now. I can't fuss at my people for being late if I show up late."

I got her to work with twenty minutes to spare, then headed back to the hotel. I grabbed all of the shit I had bought her and went back to the mall to get my money back. I would be back in Memphis before she clocked out of work. That bitch was crazy as hell if she thought I really was going to marry her ass.

Chapter 6

Demarcus

Telling Joyce everything about me from the age of thirteen to now probably wasn't the smartest thing to do, but I wanted her help. I told her about my mother's prostitution days, how and when Lord King confessed to being my father, and the bullshit I was going through with Bria. Out of all the stuff I had told her about killing Orlando and selling dog food, her first question to me was, "Do you miss playing football?"

I found it odd that she had asked me that, but she was the first and only person to have ever asked me. "Yeah, I guess I miss it. I really haven't thought about it because when I do, it makes me think—"

She cut me off to finish my sentence. "It makes you think about the rape, the jail time, and how your mama died while you were away. I can understand that."

For the first time in the two hours we had been talking, the room fell silent and uncomfortable, so I took the opportunity to question her. "So, why did Jacob send you instead of coming? Are you his partner or something?"

She laughed. "No. I wouldn't work with Jacob's no-good ass for any amount of money. He's a criminal and all of his clients are well-known drug dealers. That's why he told me about your case. Keith Willis, who you call Lord King, was being investigated, and so was Jacob, and Jacob asked me to come down yesterday to see if I would be his lawyer. After hearing everything he would possibly be charged with, I declined to represent him and was on my way back to Atlanta when he called me about your case."

"What made him call on you?"

"Besides being the best, I owe him a favor," she said, lowering her head. "My father was like Lord King and met his same fate. My brothers took over the family business, and, after years of bailing them out of trouble, I decided to go into law. My oldest brother was headed to the federal penitentiary, but Jacob made sure he never spent the night there. I am my brother's keeper, and one scratched back deserves another."

"So are you taking my case?"

She stood up and grabbed her belongings off the dining room table. "I guess so, Mr. Elder, but I need a new Benz, and I don't like car notes. Also, I need some renovations done on the house I bought my mother, and refinancing isn't the route I want to take."

"Name the price. We can go scoop your Benz in the morning. There's no price I won't pay to keep my freedom."

"I know there isn't, and I'll be back tomorrow to pick up my retainer before I head back home. Good night, Mr. Elder."

"Good night, Ms. Claybrooks."

I stood in the doorway until she pulled off my dead-end street. I slammed the door when I saw Bria turn into the Roberts' driveway. I didn't know where she was living now, but I prayed it wasn't there. Living here with her in walking distance wasn't something I could deal with.

Although, I couldn't lie. It felt good to be back in the house I'd grown up in, and I loved the changes Rico had made after we got Omar out of it. The once three-bedroom house was now two thanks to Omar, but Rico had switched it up from the club Omar had turned it into. The stage, stripper pole, and fish tank were gone, and the house looked more like a home again. He'd had expensive drapes hung,

Ashley Furniture had graced every room furniture was needed in, and the kitchen was no longer a bank with a safe. It was filled with stainless-steel Kenmore appliances. All of Omar's exits from the house had been sealed, and the surveillance cameras had been upgraded and multiplied in numbers. All I needed now were household goods. I had to make Spank bring me a roll of tissue when he brought my car so I could take a shit. I refused to stay one more night in the house without hitting up Walmart and a grocery store. If I was lucky, Walmart would have one inside of it.

After I'd spent $300 on food and another hundred on toiletries, I was unloading my bags when Bria came down the street.

"Need some help?"

"Naw, I'm good."

She was as pretty as I remembered her being, but her eyes held more pain, and she had the bags under them to prove it.

"So you moved back into your mom's house, I see."

"Yep."

"Are you going to invite me in?"

"Hell naw! For what, Bria?"

She grabbed the forty-eight pack of toilet tissue off the back seat and followed me to my front door. "So we can finally talk, Demarcus."

"You can leave the tissue on the porch. Thanks," I said, ignoring her.

"No, I'm coming in."

"Then I'm calling the police. You're trespassing."

"I wish you would call the police on me after all the shit you put me through." The words came out of her mouth hot like fire.

"You called them on me. You even had me served with a restraining order. And everything you claim I did to you, you did the shit to yourself. I didn't know you were Omar's bitch, or I wouldn't have never fucked with you to begin with."

"I'm not nor was I ever anybody's bitch, and I know you wouldn't have fucked with me." The anger was leaving her voice. "That's why I didn't tell you, Demarcus; but we can move on from all of this. We've been through a lot worse, and I love you."

"How's your drug addiction going, Bria? You know, the one you decided not to tell me about?" I wanted to sound as fucked up and coldhearted as possible. I heard the word love come out of her mouth, but I was done with love.

"I've been clean for almost two years now and am going to meetings religiously."

"But we haven't been together in three years. You're on that shit bad, I see. Well, Bria, the truth is . . ." I turned and looked deep into her eyes. I wanted to bypass every protective wall she had up and talk directly to her soul. My next words needed to pierce it. "I don't fuck with junkies unless they're spending money with me. Since I'm all out of dog food at the present moment, I suggest your needle-marked-up ass get the fuck off my property and don't come back unless you're spending money."

She stood there, staring back at me with her puppy dog eyes locked on mine. She was waiting for my eyes to soften up, but they never did.

"What happened, Bria? You changed your mind? You need to cop you a fix? I can call my nigga up to bring you some for the low, but I don't take change."

"Fuck you, Demarcus."

"We already played that game, and you lost. Now get your junkie ass off my porch before I call the police on you."

She took off crying back to the Roberts' house.

"Ay, Spank. I need you to do me a favor, but this has to stay between us."

Spank must have been in his car when I called because there was loud music blasting in the background.

"Turn that shit down!" I yelled in the phone like it was my background preventing him from hearing me.

"I can't. I'm at the strip club. Hold on a second. I'm gonna go outside."

It took him a minute or so to get to someplace quiet, but when he did I ripped it to him. "What strip club are you at? I know you're not at LK's."

"Hell yeah! Rico's throwing a good-bye party for LK tonight. Didn't you know?"

"Hell naw, I didn't know. Rico didn't tell me shit."

"Well, you told him to run shit while you're gone, so I guess he didn't think you needed to know."

I didn't think about the strip club. I had assumed, since Lord King was dead, the city would have shut it down, but that wasn't the purpose of my call. "Look, I need you to get some info on Bria for me."

"Bria? For what, nigga? She's old news."

"The bitch is living back at her uncle's house down the street, and I need to know her every move since she's able to see me every day."

"I feel you on that," he said.

"Cool, and don't tell Rico shit."

"I won't, but promise me you're not going to fuck back with her. She's no good, my nigga."

"I feel you, and I know you got my back but, Spank, my business ain't your business. Just do what I asked of you."

Weeks passed, and I hadn't seen nor heard from Bria, which was good. Spank had given me her Narcotics Anonymous schedule and he told me she was working as a peer counselor at a rehab. I felt fucked up about dogging her, but I had to show no love. Showing love when it came to Bria would have been like Superman confessing his weakness to kryptonite to everybody he got emotionally attached to. There are some things men aren't supposed to do, and wearing our emotions like a fresh white T-shirt is one of them.

I was chilling at my barbershop, chopping it up with my employees when Joyce walked in with the good news.

"You are no longer a suspect here or in Nashville. Ready to go Benz shopping? It is the day before Christmas," she said, handing me the papers that stated what she had said to me.

I flew out of my chair, picked her up off the ground, and spun her around. "Hell yeah! I'm ready."

We left her car in the parking lot and hopped in my truck. "I got a few other things to give you and talk to you about, too," she said, opening up her briefcase.

"I learned from a boss never to discuss business in a car, remember? That shit you want to talk about will have to wait."

I hit play on my CD player and a throwback Jay-Z album filled the void of sound in the car. To my surprise, she closed her briefcase and bobbed her head to the music. I pulled into Olive Garden fifteen minutes later. "I thought we could talk over a late lunch if that's cool with you?"

"That's fine, as long as you know that you're treating," she said, getting out of the pickup truck with a jump.

We were seated and eating our appetizers before the conversation started up. "There's this, and then there's this," she said, handing me a manila folder and then a once sealed envelope. I opened the folder and read through its contents. Before I could ask any questions, she was filling in the blanks.

"I don't believe Lord King knew he wasn't your biological father. He wrote his will in the early nineties and had already left you everything he owned. Although you won't get his houses because they found proof he'd purchased them with drug money, the club is yours. It was his grandfather's, and it used to be—"

"A barbershop back in the day," I completed her sentence.

"Right. A barbershop with a nice-size parking lot he used to rent to the neighboring businesses for their customers to use. The drug task force seized his homes and cleaned them out, but Detective Rawlings thought it was only right that you got to keep this," she said, opening her briefcase and handing me a manila envelope marked EVIDENCE.

I opened it and dropped everything that was inside of it as soon as I realized what it was. The envelope was filled with pictures of my mama and Lord King. Not only amateur pictures but professional ones as well. I flipped through all of them, and the last one damn near broke me down. There was a picture of my mom, Lord King, and me standing outside the Lorraine Motel, where Martin Luther King Jr. was killed.

"Turn it over. You need to read the back," Joyce instructed.

I recognized my mama's writing before I read what it said:

> *Keith,*
> *I want you to have this picture, so you*
> *can see what a real family looks like. This*
> *is what I want for Demarcus, but having a*

*father who's running numbers and selling
drugs is preventing that. Hold on to this
picture because this will be the last time
you see him. If you come back around us,
I'm going to the police. Tough love from
me is better than no love from me, and I
choose to continue to love you.*

   Sharon

I was speechless, and the frog in my throat
wouldn't have let me speak if I had tried to.
There was the proof that I needed to set me back
right with Lord King. He wasn't using me to get
his money; he thought I was son and had died
thinking I was his son. A part of me wondered
if my mama had known he wasn't my father
and was one of those trifling, *Maury*-going-on
bitches trying to pin a baby on him. But knowing
I would never get the answer to that, I left well
enough alone and opened the other envelope.

   To Whom It May Concern:
   *My sister was raped and killed by her
john, which was the fast-money lifestyle
she introduced me to, and I'm done with it.
Demarcus Elder didn't rape me. My sister
thought we could get money out of him
and his family if we set him up. I came into*

the hotel with plans to seduce him, and it worked. My sister told me all I had to do was get him to put his semen in me, and we would get some of his signing bonus from his football career, but everything backfired on us.

When we decided to approach him for money and we had shared our plans with a friend, we found out that college football players don't get paid for playing. We then reached out to the club owner who was rumored to be a close family member, and he only paid my sister half of what she asked for, so she took me to the emergency room and had the rape kit done.

I was young and didn't know any better then. It wasn't until I saw the news that I realized how bad I had ruined Demarcus's life. When I saw him at his cell phone store last month, it made me wonder how far his career would have gone if we wouldn't have interfered with it. Two days after seeing him, I got the news of my sister . . .

I stopped reading the letter right there. "What the fuck is this supposed to prove? Did you have something to do with her writing this?"

Joyce's mouth opened in shock. "No. I didn't have anything to do with this, Demarcus. She sent a copy of this letter to the courts and Jacob, and Jacob forwarded his copy to me. This changes a lot for you. I thought you'd be happy."

"Happy? I'm supposed to be happy that the bitch came out and said the same thing that I told the courts? That didn't stop me from serving twenty-two months or from being registered as a sex offender. Naw, this bullshit doesn't make me happy. It doesn't give me my time back."

I had gotten loud, and Joyce attempted to get me to lower my voice by whispering her next words: "This could change a lot for you. How do you not see that?"

"What will it change? Don't you know Tennessee's statute of limitations for statutory rape? I was eighteen, and the bitch was fourteen."

Joyce laughed.

"What the fuck is funny?"

"I'm laughing because you think you know more about the law than me. I didn't mean to hit a nerve. Look, I can file a petition with the courts on your behalf with the new evidence, and it will cost you a little bit of nothing—"

"Oh, so that's what this shit is about? Money?" I cut her off.

"No, but I don't work for free."

I stood up and pulled a hundred dollars off of my money clip and set it on the table. "I'm not hungry anymore, but I'm sure you are. I just don't think food will feed your type of hunger."

"What are you saying, Demarcus?"

"I'm saying get your money-hungry ass up so you can get your pay; and I liked it better when you called me Mr. Elder."

"I understand, Mr. Elder."

We got in the truck silently, and I went to the bank and got a $60,000 cashier's check. Instead of taking her to the car lot, I dropped her ass off back at her car and smashed off on her. I wanted to paddleboat in a bottle of liquor, with blunts as the anchor preventing me from drifting, but instead I drove to the community center.

The signs on the door led me into the gym for family night. I didn't know why I went, but it was too late to turn around.

"Before we go into introductions, I have an announcement to make." The guy standing behind the microphone was shaking like a leaf but he wore a big smile on his yellow face. I guessed he was in his early forties, not because his face looked older but because of his receding hairline and the sprinkles of gray in his beard. I could tell he worked out or, at least, did some bodybuilding by the cuts of his arms seeping through his sweater. A woman who was around his same age walked on the stage and stood next to him.

"You all know my wife and I met right here in this gym ten years ago as addicts. We came here as individuals trying to get help, and we fell in love. Well, I'm happy to announce that, after ten years clean and eight years of marriage, we are expecting our first child. Deborah is three months pregnant!"

The gym fell into an uproar of applause mixed with yells of "Congratulations!" Once the room had calmed down, the people went around introducing themselves. They stated their names, said they were an addict as well, and named their drug or drugs of choice and how long they had been clean. After that, they announced the guest they had brought with them. Bria hadn't stood up; she let the couple next to her skip her, and the guy holding the microphone made sure to call her out on it.

"Bria, you came alone again? What happened to your uncle? He used to be your support."

Bria stood up, ready to explain Mr. Roberts's absence to a roomful of people with their eyes on her, but I didn't give her the chance.

"I'm here in her uncle's place today."

All eyes transferred from her to me, and Bria's eyes filled with tears. I walked over to her and grabbed her hand.

"Welcome. And you are?" the director asked into the microphone, but he didn't seem happy that Bria had someone there for her.

"I'm Demarcus, Bria's ex-fiancé."

"Oh, okay." He turned his attention back to Bria. "Bria, are you okay with him being here? I know in our one-on-one sessions he has come up in a not-so-good light."

I wanted to ask what was said, but I let it go and waited for her response.

"I'm fine with him being here, perfectly fine," she said with a smile as she wiped away her tears. "I guess it's my turn then. My name is Bria, and I am a heroin addict. I have been clean for twenty-one months and twenty-seven days. My guest for family night is Mr. Demarcus Elder."

"Of Dee's Communications?" a male voice yelled out.

"Yes, that very same one," Bria said as the room welcomed me.

That went well, I guessed. I got to hear first-hand how different drugs had fucked people up; but, to be honest, listening to all those tearjerk-ers wouldn't make me hang up my hat selling them. I was planning my retirement from the game to run my legit businesses, not because of how dog food fucked up lives.

When the meeting was over, I was approached by different people wanting information on how to get a phone with bad credit, so I gave out a few business cards. I hadn't come to network but, hell, I still didn't know why I had shown up.

"Can I get a ride home?" Bria asked with a smile.

"Sure, but where's your car?"

"In the shop. My transmission went out a week ago, and they want too much to fix it, so I've been paying people to get around until I save up to get it fixed or for a down payment on something new."

Bria rode all the way home without attempting to hold a conversation, like we had an unspoken form of communication, and she knew I wasn't in the mood. I passed up her house and pulled into my driveway, and she didn't say a word. She got out and started heading to her house, but I ran up behind her and grabbed her hand. I led her into my house and to my room, and she got undressed without saying a word. I fell asleep with all of me inside of her and, when I woke up, she was gone. There was a plate of breakfast on my nightstand with a note that read, "Merry Christmas, Dee," next to it. I couldn't help but smile.

I stayed in bed all day watching Christmas parades and movies. I wanted to reach out to Bria, but I wasn't in the mood to discuss whatever she felt like we needed to discuss, so I smoked a blunt and went to sleep. Spank came through around nine o'clock at night to bring me a plate of Christmas dinner his mom had made me, and as I walked him out to his car I noticed Bria had her car back.

I tried to call her, but her cell went straight to voicemail twice, like it was dead. I debated on going down there once Spank was out of sight and said fuck it and went. When I made it to her car in the driveway, Bria had a mouthful of the NA director's dick as he finger banged her with his eyes closed. They hadn't seen me watching, and I had been standing there a few minutes. The longer I watched her head bob up and down in his lap, the more I could feel my heart kicking out of it any feelings I had left for her. This was exactly what I needed to get over her. I smiled as I walked off and said, "Fuck Bria."

Leaving the shit at that would have been the old me, but the new me walked around that motherfucka, snatched the door open, pushed Bria to the side, and went to work on buddy. I hit him so many times that I had to look behind me to make sure that I was the only one throw-

ing punches at him. Bria was screaming at me
to stop, but this fist-to-face conversation was
needed between us men. Once the dazed look
crossed his face, I yanked him out of the car,
making him hit the concrete. I wanted to keep
whooping his ass, but his overly buff ass wasn't
any competition for me, and I felt like I was
beating on the handicapped. I walked off as Bria
lay next to him, nursing his wounds.

When I made it to my front door, Bria was
running up behind me, screaming at me, "What
the fuck is wrong with you, Demarcus? He got
my car out the shop, and I owed him money.
That was it. He doesn't mean shit to me."

I tried to keep walking, but when she grabbed
me by my left arm, my reflexes kicked in. I
backhanded Bria across her face, and she hit
the steps and flipped back down them. I went
in the house and closed the door behind me but
not before I heard her say, "So you think you're
Omar now, nigga?"

*If the bitch only knew how bad I want to put
a bullet in her, she'd leave me the fuck alone
right now.*

Chapter 7

Omar

"Beat his ass, little cousin."

I had a front-row seat to the best boxing match of the year. Demarcus was beating the shit out of some nigga Bria had in the car with her. I was parked at the entrance of the cul-de-sac but had a good view of what was going on. I had only been in Memphis for a few weeks, but it was hell getting another car, so I ended up keeping Unique's until three days ago. I knew she had reported her car stolen by now, and if she ran her mouth like I knew she would then I was sure the police had informed her that the SUV I'd left her was registered to a murder victim back in Detroit. She knew my first name, but not my real last name; but I was sure she'd told them we went to the mall, so they could pull the surveillance video or, better yet, she pulled the one of me at her job when I first made it back to Louisville. I didn't give a fuck, though; I knew my days were numbered. I'd either be dead or sitting in a jail cell for life, but either way it went I was going to get my body count up before I met either fate.

Demarcus still looked like me, but he was the big cousin now. He had put on about thirty pounds since I had last seen him, and although he was only wearing a T-shirt and sweats, he had a swag about him that looked like money. He had a goatee, and I was rocking a Billy goat and was now a full-fledged member of the beard gang. It was a Detroit thing to let your chin hair grow long with a Caesar, and I was feeling the look. It looked better on me than those niggas up North anyways.

I watched as that ho Bria went running down the block behind Demarcus; and when she caught up to him, he put fire to her ass. I didn't know what it was about Bria that made you want to slap the shit out of her, but she was definitely one of those bitches you had to put your hands on. The sick part about it was that Bria would fall in love and want you more after you'd hit her. Demarcus didn't know it, but he was going to catch hell trying to get rid of her now; but, being the good nigga I was, I volunteered to help him out. I'd seen the Robertses leave yesterday, and they hadn't returned, which meant the bitch was home alone. Once the wimp she had with her pulled off with his pride stuck on Demarcus's fist, I met Bria on her porch.

"What's up, baby? Did you miss me?"

Demarcus's handprint had left a red mark on her face, but it didn't cover up the fear mixed with shock that crossed it when she saw me. "Omar, please leave. The police are already on their way."

I knew she was lying, but I'd play the game with her. "Okay, well, I'll wait for them to come. I'll be your witness, baby. I saw my bitch-ass cousin put his hands on you. Let me see your face."

Bria jumped when I reached out my hand.

"Come on now, baby. I'm not going to hit you."

She stuck her hand in her pocket and tried to power on her phone without me noticing it, but she was caught red-handed. I took the phone from her, put it in my pocket, and threw her ass in the house for a Christmas nut.

Bria put up a fight, which I wasn't ready for. As I locked the door, I felt the baseball bat hit my back, but there wasn't enough force behind it to cause me any real damage. I snatched it out of her hand and cracked her across her rib cage with it.

"That shit doesn't feel good, does it?"

She screamed in pain. "What do you want, Omar?"

"What I always want, baby. I want you."

"I'm with Demarcus now."

"That's not what his handprint across your face is saying. Looks to me like he just called whatever it was y'all had quits."

"It's not quits. We just had a misunderstanding. You should leave before he gets back."

"Oh, is he coming like you said the police are? Bitch, please. He don't love you like I do. He's not about to chase your ass."

"He loves me more than you ever did, and I love him more than I ever loved you."

I slapped the taste of her last words out of her mouth, then locked my hands around her throat. "So you thought you could just say fuck me and fall in love with my little cousin, and I wouldn't do shit about it? I told you years ago, Bria, 'Once mine, always mine,' didn't I?"

She tried to nod her head, but my grip around her throat wouldn't allow her to move it.

"Now, give me a kiss."

I stuck my tongue in her mouth; and after a few seconds she was really kissing me back like she loved me, so I released the hold I had on her neck and wrapped my hands around her waist.

"Now, that's better, baby. You know you love me. I don't know why you tried to put up a fight." I let her go and unbuckled my pants. "You know he missed you, don't you?"

She nodded her head while rubbing her sore throat.

"It's Christmas, baby. Get on your knees and give daddy a present."

She got on her knees, and I let my pants drop. She took me in her mouth, and I lost all the feelings in my toes. She had that vacuum cleaner suction and, if my memory served me right, she would suck my babies out of me if I didn't stop her and get the pussy first. But I wanted to feel her for a little bit longer. Bria slowed down her bob and then sank her teeth into my meat. At the last second, she changed her mind about biting me, but I had felt the sharpness of her teeth, so it was too late.

"Stupid bitch!" I bellowed out as I gave her two quick blows to her face with my fist. Bria fell back to the floor, dazed, and then I attacked her.

"You tried to bite my dick, bitch! I see you want to play me. Did you forget who I am and what I'll do to you?"

I hit her with multiple combos. Her face was now the speed bag, and I was the boxer preparing for fight night. Blood flew from her mouth and nose with each punch that landed. Then, her left eye closed. Bria dug her nails into the sides of my stomach, but I was too mad to feel the pain of my skin being ripped off.

"Take these motherfucking pants off!"

I told her to do it, but I was already snatching them off of her. Bria was fading in and out of consciousness and wouldn't have been able to take them off anyway. I placed my left hand around her neck and spat in my right. Somebody had to get my dick hard. I stroked my meat until it rocked up like cocaine and then I rammed into her desert that had replaced the normal wetlands between her thighs. It felt like I was fucking sandpaper, and I was getting the dick burns to prove it. I looked up at Bria, and the tears rolling down her face said she agreed with me; the shit hurt. I pulled back out of her and spat directly on my meat. I tried to no-hand my way back inside of her, but I was knocked over.

"Die, you sick bastard!" Bria screamed as she continued to beat me all over my body with the bat.

I let her hit me two more times, once in the ribs and the other to the back of my head. After that, I played dead on her ass. She dropped the bat and ran to the house phone. She managed to dial five digits before I snatched the line out of the wall and picked up that damn baseball bat she seemed to love. Bria ran up the stairs to the second floor, taking two steps at a time. I couldn't keep up with her; everything on my body hurt. I was sure she had broken a few of my ribs because it was hard for me to breathe, and the hit to my head not only gave me a killer headache, but I was seeing double, too.

When I made it upstairs, Bria had locked herself in the hallway bathroom. I didn't know if she had a phone in there with her, so I headed back downstairs to make my escape; but I noticed the bedroom next to the bathroom. It had an entrance to the hallway bathroom connected to it. It only took a second to see the lock on the handle had been switched. Instead of being able to lock the door while in the bathroom, the lock was in the bedroom preventing those using the bathroom from entering the bedroom. I walked in on Bria curled up in a ball on the floor. She was using a washrag to catch the blood from her nose and a pair of scissors was in her free hand.

"Please, Omar. I'm done fighting."

I cocked the baseball bat over my shoulder and then hit a home run. Blood shot out from the top of the right side of Bria's head, and she fell over on her stomach. She was still alive, but death was coming. With her lying there facedown and naked below the waist, I took advantage of my leverage.

"I'm getting my nut. Fuck what you thought!"

I grabbed the hand soap and glazed my meat. It was hard for me to get on the floor, but I used the bat as a crutch to get me down there. I set the bat on the back of Bria's neck, and then I beat my meat. Bria was shaking and jerking on the floor, which made it hard for me to get it up, but I managed. I shoved my half-inflated meat into her tight exit that she always played stingy with and I went to work.

"I told you, 'Once mine, always mine,' but then you go and fuck my cousin. You hurt me, Bria."

With every stroke, pain from my ribs shot through me, so I rested my hands on both ends of the bat to even out my weight and give me some relief. The pressure I had on the bat dug into Bria's neck, causing it to crack as I released my never-to-be-born kids into their new shithole of a home. *Now that's what I call good-bye sex!*

When I was done getting my proper closure from Bria, I was too tired to handle my business with Demarcus, and the car in his driveway was gone. I drove around until I found a prostitute and then I paid her a hundred dollars to get me a motel in her name on the south side of the city. I had to move fast, and I knew just who I needed to find to help me out.

I waited until the morning to go on my hunt. I went to all his known hangouts but I didn't find him anywhere. I almost drove right by him because I had never seen him doing manual labor before.

"What's up, Unc?"

Uncle Leroy stopped hauling the trash that was filled with opened, empty Christmas presents and torn-up boxes and he just stared at me for a second. "I really gotta stop shooting that shit up. It has me seeing ghosts and shit," he said out loud and then he returned to what he was doing.

"I'm no ghost, Unc. You looking at your favorite nephew, live in the flesh."

Uncle Leroy let go of the trashcan and took off running down the street. I jumped out and chased him two city blocks before he stopped. I snatched his ass up. "Why in the fuck did you run, nigga?"

He was out of breath. "They said you were dead, nigga. I thought zombies had attacked Memphis. Look at you. You're small, ashy, and dirty. When's the last time you washed your ass, nigga? You look dead."

"I'm in costume. I'm trying to look smoked out like you."

"It's working," he said, looking me up and down. "What do you want with me? Demarcus is gonna kill you when he finds out you're still alive."

"Not if I kill him and Lord King first, and you're the nigga who's going to help me do it."

"No, I'm not. Dee has been good to me, and this is his city now. Lord King is already dead; he and Killa went at it, and now both of those niggas is fertilizer. Everything is different now. I'm in rehab trying to get myself together. I've changed. I don't do illegal shit anymore. I'm a born-again Christian."

"Oh, I get it. You thought I was giving your bitch ass an option, huh? Naw, this shit ain't negotiable. You sold me out to Dee, and if Killa and JP weren't so money hungry, I'd be dead too. I need a life for a life. Here goes a little extra." I handed him a fifty dollar bill, but he didn't take it.

"I'm not doing it, Omar, so you can kill me now. Dee has already been through too much. If you want to get him, you're on that mission by yourself. Put your money away. I told you, I'm clean."

I snatched the nigga up by his jacket and dug in his pockets. He had two dollars in change in one and a homemade needle and lighter in the other.

"So you're clean?"

"Hell naw, I ain't clean. Who told you that bullshit? But I'm not an accessory to murder. You can bet your dick and balls on that one."

I pulled out my gun. "You are now, nigga. Now get to walking."

"Omar, go ahead and kill me. I ain't selling Demarcus out to you. You've been fucking with that boy all of his life. Leave him alone. The whole family fucked him over, including his mama. Give the boy a break. Damn!"

"He provoked me."

"No, he didn't. You've had it out for him since diaper days. I'm not helping you get him, so kill me like you plan on doing. I've been trying to get to heaven anyways, but these buses don't run that way. Put me out of my misery. I'm ready to chill with my mama and my nieces, and pimp hoes in heaven."

Uncle Leroy closed his eyes and crossed his hands over his chest like a mummy. I wanted to kill him, but I needed him to be my informant. He had already told me shit I didn't know about Lord King being dead. I knew there was more information to get out of him.

"I'm not going to kill you, Uncle. We're family; but you're going to help me do this, whether you like it or not. I'm giving you fifty dollars and a gram of dog food now. I'll give you five hundred dollars more and some more food when you tell me what all you know. You don't have to set him up. I just need info."

He opened one of his eyes. "Can I think about it? I mean, give me the fifty dollars today, and I'll call tomorrow with my answer. If I don't have to set him up, we might be able to work something out."

"Who do you think you're talking to, Unc? If I give you the money, I'm not going to hear from you, and I don't have time to waste. I'll come back tomorrow at the same time. Meet me right here." I tore the bill in half and gave him a piece. "You'll get the rest tomorrow."

He took the torn bill. "What about the boy? You said you'd give me some of that, too."

"You'll get that tomorrow if you show up."

I walked off on him and got back in the car. I didn't have anywhere to go, and I didn't want to reach out to the people I knew because I knew them from working for Lord King. Sitting in the motel was out of the question, too. I drove down Jackson, past the Department of Human Services, into Little Mexico. When I wanted some good weed, I'd get it from a Mexican named Carlos in exchange for some dog food. He didn't shoot it up, but he sold it.

"What's up, Carlos?"

Carlos was sitting in front of his tire shop covered in grease and oil. He was the go-to man of the Latino community, and I had met him on a whim. I needed to get off the dummy tire I had been riding on, and his was the first tire shop I had passed. I smoked my blunt while he switched out my tire, and he told me I was smoking on bullshit and he gave me what he was smoking. After that, he became my new weed man.

"Damn! Look what the cat dragged in. Where you been, Omar? You look fucked up."

That's what I loved about Mexicans; they didn't bite their tongues for shit.

"I've been staying low and keeping my nose clean, but I need that good you got."

Carlos took off his nonprescription glasses that he wore to hide his boss status with a nerd look and said, "Follow me, my friend."

We went into his office, where he weighed me out an ounce. "That's all you need today, amigo?"

I hesitated asking for it, but fuck it. I needed it to pay Uncle Leroy with. "And let me get two grams of that *monteca*."

Monteca means "butter" in Spanish, which was their slang word for heroin. I had never copped any from him, but he was about his money, and he served me without question.

When I got in the car, I unwrapped the dog food and held it in my hand for a second. I could tell his product was good just by touching it. Since I was already on that side of town, I got me a plate of tacos and went back to the motel. I hadn't realized it, but I still had the mushed dog food in my hand when I sat down to eat.

I didn't want it to go to waste, so I rubbed it on the inside of my rolling paper and then added the weed on top of it. I wasn't addicted to the shit, but after fucking Symphony with it on my dick for so long, I needed a fix every now and then. It was a pick-me-up, not an addiction. I wasn't shooting it up nor was I using it frequently, but I'd have me a taste when I was feeling low.

I smoked a fourth of the blunt and then put it out. It wasn't as potent as the dog food I served because I'd let my body heat warm it up. Heroin had to be stored in cool, dry areas to keep its power, so I made sure to always kill its potency with the heat and sweat of my palms. I was feeling good, and the pain from Bria's beating the night before had temporarily disappeared. I wanted some pussy more than the tacos that sat in front of me, so I posted on the motel's balcony. First ho I saw selling pussy was about to get the dicking of her life.

It took thirty minutes before I saw a white bitch come out of a room looking like she had just finished serving somebody else, but she was ready to make some more money.

"What did you say your name was again?"

"Call me Sapphire, baby. If you don't mind, I'm going to take a shower first, and then I'll be right with you."

I lit the blunt back up as I waited with my steel in my free hand. It was taking Sapphire too damn long, so I walked in the bathroom on her ass, and she was doing a line of cocaine.

"Hurry up, baby. Daddy needs this nut."

"I'm coming, but if you want the ride of your life let me finish powdering my nose first. Sapphire is going to take good care of you, daddy."

"That's what the fuck I'm talking about," I said while stroking my dick.

She was already naked, and I could see her nipples getting hard. I wasn't into fucking women who didn't have any meat on their bones, but Sapphire was a working girl, so I knew she'd handle her business right. When she saw me stroking my meat, she began playing between the thin lips she had between her legs.

"You ready?" I said.

"Yeah, I'm ready, daddy. It's seventy-five dollars if you want head, too, and if you plan on not using a condom it'll be a hundred."

I didn't have a condom, but I didn't want to pay her ass a hundred. I never spent more than fifty dollars on a prostitute of her caliber, but I needed it. "You're busting my head with them high-ass prices, but come on. And that mouth of yours better be good."

Her mouth was better than good, and she kept my balls occupied, too. I hadn't had any head in a long time that made me want to eat some cat, but she had earned it. I sat her on the toilet with one leg propped up on the wall and the other on the sink and then put my tongue to work. She tasted like water, and that was exactly what I needed to quench my thirst. I tongue kissed her erect clit like the bitch was mine, and she made sure to cover my mouth in her juices. I stood up and pushed her head back, causing it to hit the back of the toilet; and then I put my steel inside of her. She was doing some strange shit with her muscles that caused me to pull out of her and put my meat in her mouth. I busted my first one in seconds, and she swallowed all of it. She started getting up like I was done.

"It ain't over yet, Sapphire. That was the pre-game show."

I picked her up and wrapped the bones she had for legs around my waist and put myself back inside of her. I hit her all the way to the bed.

She rested her knees on her shoulders and let me dig her out. She was loud and screaming like she was a virgin.

"Daddy's big dick's good, huh?"

"Hell yeah," she said over and over again. "Daddy got some good big dick."

I looked up at her face, and she was beautiful. The years of drug abuse and self-destruction were etched on her face, but it couldn't hide her beauty. I didn't know if it was the heroin talking, but with a little tender loving care she could be bad again. Her sex game was off the charts, and she was begging for anal. I liked a woman who knew where all her pleasure points were and wasn't scared to share them. We went at it for another forty-five minutes, and it would have been longer, but she said some shit I wasn't ready for.

"Spray it on me, daddy. Paint my body."

I didn't have time to think about it because it shot out of me like an aerosol can. She played in it for a while and then licked it off her fingers.

"Damn, girl," I said, shaking out my legs, trying to stretch them out before they cramped up on me.

"What happened to you, daddy? You're all cut and bruised up."

I hadn't forgotten about the beating that had been put on me but I was in no mood to talk about it. "I'm good, baby. Come get your sexy ass in the shower with me and help me clean my wounds."

We washed our bodies, and she cleaned my wounds. I jumped when she touched them, and she fell on her knees to make it up to me. "This one is free."

The water was hitting her face, but she acted as if it wasn't there. When she got me back at attention, she bent over and gave me round three. Sapphire did another line as I dressed.

"So how do I get you to be mine?"

"I have a lot of returning customers. I'll give you my number, so you can call me when you need to."

"I don't mean as a customer. I want to take you out shopping or something from time to time. Maybe we can kick it without the sex."

She finished her line and got dressed in a hurry. "That's not how this works, baby. I'm always on the clock."

"So you're saying the only time I can spend time with you is when I'm paying for the pussy?"

"Right, and I need my hundred dollars now. I have other customers waiting."

"What if I'm not ready for you to leave yet? Can I give you fifty dollars to stay and chill with me for an hour or so?"

"Hell no. In an hour, I can make way more than that. Listen, sweetie, I run across men like you all the time who confuse me doing my job with something else. If you're looking for a companion, call an escort service. I'm selling pussy, not time. Now where's my money?"

"I'm not giving you shit," I said, lighting up my blunt.

She pulled out a box cutter. "Give me my money."

I pulled out my gun and snatched a pillow off the bed. "Come and get it."

She took a step toward me, and I shot her through the pillow somewhere between her chest and stomach. Before the blood could hit the carpet, I grabbed her and put her in the tub portion of the shower. She was still alive, so I went back in the room and grabbed her box cutter. The blade on it was dull, but it would get the job done. I slit both of her wrists and then her neck. Blood filled the tub as I turned on the cold water.

The pillow wasn't as good a silencer as portrayed in movies, so I grabbed a cigarette and smoked it on the balcony to see if anyone had heard anything. When the first cancer stick went out, I sparked up another until the coast was clear. I went back in the room and grabbed my car keys. *Three ten-pound bags of ice should do the trick until I'm ready to make my next move.* I prayed Uncle Leroy wasn't bullshitting. My time to get Demarcus had just gotten shorter.

Chapter 8

Demarcus

Every time I thought the storm was over, another flash flood came to bring me back to reality. I was back in the interrogation room with flames of fire shooting from my nose. Joyce told me I had been cleared as a suspect in all the murders. *But I wouldn't be sitting in this chair if that were true.* My guess was that she'd turned snitch after I'd checked her ass in the restaurant.

"What's new with you, Dee? I know it's not professional to be calling you that, but after spending so much time with you recently, it feels like we're old friends. Doesn't it, Ryu?"

"Good friends," Ryu chimed in, starting the same routine they'd used the last time they'd interrogated me. "Almost like we're childhood buddies."

"Naw, it doesn't feel like that to me. It feels like police harassment at this point!" I snapped.

"No harassment here, Mr. Elder. It's just seems like you keep coming up in all of the murders that come across our desk. I wonder why that is. Do you want to take a guess at it, partner?" Ryu said, looking at Rawlings.

"Don't mind if I do, partner," Rawlings said with his eyes on me. "I think our good friend Dee here is living foul behind those TV commercials. Besides helping people get affordable cell phones in the community and the best fades in town, I think Dee has a thing for murder."

"Let's hurry this shit up, fellas. It's New Year's Eve, and I have pussy to get into, which I'm sure you faggots know nothing about!" I laughed.

"He's right, Ryu. I hate to admit it, but Dee seems to get way more pussy than us."

"You're right, partner. I settled for marriage and making love to one woman, while Mr. Elder here takes everything that comes his way. Isn't that right, Mr. Elder?"

"I don't agree that I'm taking everything that's being offered, but I have a variety of choices, so what do y'all want with me?"

"Come on, Dee. If the woman says no, you take it, or so I read in your file," Rawlings said, fumbling through a folder.

"That bitch lied on me, and I got the letter to prove it. Is that what this shit is about?"

"What about this bitch? Is she lying on you too?" Rawlings asked as he placed crime scene pictures in front of me.

At first glance, the woman wasn't recognizable because her head had swollen to twice its usually size and her face had been badly beaten. But when he laid down the pictures of her on her stomach, I knew it was Bria. I snatched all the pictures off the table and went through them with tears streaming from my eyes.

"Who did this to her? If that drug counselor had anything to do with this, that nigga is dead!" My heart burned, and I was drowning in my own tears as hate filled me. I didn't care how much the hit would cost me, but whoever had done it would die before the police could make an arrest.

"What drug counselor are you talking about? Richard?" Detective Ryu asked me.

"I don't know the nigga's name, but he ran the NA classes. I should have killed the nigga when I had the chance to!" Down came more tears out of my eyes.

"After you beat him up for getting oral from Bria or after you hit her for defending him?" Rawlings asked.

"I should have killed him when I caught him with her!" I was pissed and didn't care what I was saying. Bria had been brutally murdered, and I couldn't stop looking at her battered pictures.

"Is that what happened, Mr. Elder? You sodomized Bria, cracked her head open with a bat, then used it to break her neck because she wanted to suck on somebody other than you?" Ryu pulled out a pen before finishing. "If that's how it happened, I just need a signed confession saying it."

"Rawlings, get your partner before he earns himself a departmental funeral. I didn't kill Bria. I loved her. I beat the shit out of the counselor for treating her like she was a ho. I did slap Bria, and I was wrong for it, but she tried to justify what she had done, and it was a reflex."

"So was killing her, wasn't it, Demarcus? If you didn't kill her, where were you Christmas night and the days that followed? The streets have been filled with uniforms and crime scene investigators, but no one has seen you. If it weren't for you running that red light this morning, we wouldn't have been able to reach you." Rawlings had too much victory in his voice.

"I changed my number. I had unwanted motherfuckas calling me, like you. And I was shacked up Christmas night. I stayed with ol' girl until this morning at the Residence Inn on Madison."

"What's the name of the girl you were with?" Ryu said, ready to write down a name.

"None of your fucking business, but we sat in the lobby joking with the staff all night. If you want to check out my alibi, go there. I'm gone!" I stood up, but my eyes were scanning the pictures of Bria, looking for any signs or evidence of who murdered her.

"Not so fast, Mr. Elder. We have enough motive and opportunity to keep you in custody until we check out your alibi."

"But you don't have the DNA to match what was found under the victim's nails and in her rectum. It's nice to see you again, Detectives," Joyce said as she walked in the room. "Check out his whereabouts on the night in question and give me a call if you need to question him further. The victim was once my client's fiancée, and he is more than willing to help out with any information that will help your investigation; but, as for now, he needs time to grieve. Rawlings, have you've been working out? You're looking slimmer. Or are you stressed out from the lack of cases you've yet to solve? Let's go, Mr. Elder. Say good-bye!"

I didn't say shit. I just followed Joyce out as I had done before. Instead of getting in the car with her, I jumped in mine and headed to the house I'd inherited from Gutta.

As the door of my garage closed, the headlights on the front of Joyce's new Benz crept under the door.

"What?" I asked.

"Do you want me to take your case or not?" she asked, rolling her eyes.

"I'm not buying you another Benz!"

"That's fine. I'll settle for a pair of diamond earrings and a mini-vacation in Georgia instead."

"Cool. There isn't anything to talk about this time. I didn't do it, and I have witnesses who saw me at the hotel," I said.

"Great! But I'll still need more information, just in case anything weird pops up. They're going to come after you again since they have an eyewitness who puts you at the murder scene, and one who saw you assault the victim hours before her death. I'll only need you for a week."

"What do you mean a week?"

"Do you want me on your side or not? If you do, go pack. You'll be in Atlanta with me for a week."

"I don't do Atlanta. Bad experience!" All I wanted to do was go in the house and grieve, but Joyce was interfering with that.

"How long are you going to let your past dictate your future? Go pack, Mr. Elder. I'm fed up with your self-pity shit!" Joyce was beyond frustrated, and I was enjoying the fight she had in her. Hell, I needed the company anyway.

"Shit, if we're going to the A, I don't need to pack. I'll shop there, but how did you know I needed you?"

She smiled at me. "When they couldn't find you, they called me to bring you in. Now hurry up before we miss the countdown to the New Year."

My phone rang. "Who's this?"

The call came in private, and the only reason I had answered it was because of this Bria case. Whoever was on the other end of the phone had a bad connection, and all I could hear was a man's voice repeating my name. I hung up.

"Give me a second, Ms. Claybrooks. Pull your bucket into my garage, so we can ride in style."

I raised the garage door, exposing my Maybach as I went into the house. I thought about telling Rico or Spank that I was leaving, but I had a change of heart. I needed this getaway, and Rico loved being the biggest drug dealer in Memphis. He didn't need my help. I hadn't made it official with all the bullshit going on, but the game was his. He'd have to break bread since it was my supplies and money he was using, but I'd be willing to let him buy me out. When all of the drama disappeared, I'd take over the strip club, too. It was the biggest one we had here, so it would be stupid of me to shut it down, but there definitely would be some changes made.

As I was grabbing my shaving kit, the house phone rang. "Hello?"

"Hello. Is this Demarcus?" an unfamiliar man's voice came through the phone.

"Yeah, this is him. Who is this?"

"Hold on for a second, little bruh." There was a small pause.

"Demarcus, please don't hang up. I have something important I need to talk to you about." It was a woman's voice on the line now.

"Who is this?"

There was another pause. "Someone who has hurt you in the past and is willing to do anything to make it right."

"Look, I don't have time for guessing games. Tell me who you are, or I'm hanging up."

"Demarcus, listen. There's this guy who wants to meet with you. He found me when he Googled you. He threatened to hurt me if I didn't help him get in contact with you and go along with his plan, so I—"

I stopped her in her tracks. "Who in the fuck is this?"

"It's Sierra, Demarcus, but it's not—"

I hung up. I had my number listed in the phone book because no one used house phones anymore, so I thought they wouldn't take the time to look me up. With me being a sex offender, the state probably kept the victim updated with my information. I guessed that was how she found me. She wasn't a victim, but that was what the shit said on paper, and I couldn't dispute it. I should have heard her out first because now I was left with puzzle pieces to try to put together without a picture to go by. I pressed *69 but got a busy signal. I'd give her my full attention if she called back.

"What's wrong, Mr. Elder?" Joyce asked when I made it back to my car. She had worry written on her face.

"It just hit me that I'll be ringing in the New Year in Atlanta with you. Mom Dukes used to say whoever you ring in the year with is who you'll spend it with."

"Then, I guess you'll be in and out of jail all year. I hope Mom Dukes is right. I need the money!" She could have died from laughing.

I pulled off and hit the highway. I hadn't really checked Joyce out. Once I saw her dreads, I was instantly not interested. I wasn't a weave man, but I wasn't fond of women with dreads, either. I wanted to be able to comb my fingers through a woman's hair as I dug into her from the back. Holding entwined balls of naps wasn't sexy to me at all. I don't like women with fake braids, either. I'd give a second look to a bitch with an afro before either one of those hairstyles.

I got my first good look at her when we stopped to get gas in Alabama. She was walking away from the pump, and her ass looked like it was seconds away from tearing through her pants like the Hulk. Her dreads were long and fell to the middle of her back. I instantly got a visualization of me hitting that donkey from the back while holding on to her dreads like reins. She was cute, too. There wasn't anything on her face that stood out, but she was far from ugly. I wasn't trying to be a pervert, but if I was looking I might as well check out everything, and that print in her pants was fat. I hadn't seen a camel toe that fat since my eighth grade math teacher's, and I wanted to bite it. Moving my eyes up some more, I saw she had C-cups, and when I made it back up to her face, she was staring right at me.

"Did you find whatever it was you were looking for?"

"Yeah, I did," I said, wearing a smirk on my face.

"I'm glad, but do me a favor. Keep your findings to yourself. You hear?"

"Yes, ma'am."

I thought Joyce might be a lesbian. She didn't have a ring on her finger, and I hadn't heard her mention having a man in her life. She told me she was the only girl in her family, and being around nothing but men can do that to a woman. If she was playing for the home team, she wasn't batting. She was too feminine to be anybody's stud, but with her living in Atlanta, one could never tell, so I fed her a line.

"Your man isn't going to try to start any shit with me for ringing in the year with you, is he? I'd hate to have to fuck buddy up!"

She smiled at me, showing all her pretty white teeth, and then said, "No. I got rid of his ass two years ago, but if he were still in the picture, your scrawny ass wouldn't have a chance up against him."

"Oh, so you're into those steroid-taking, extra-thick-neck-having niggas, huh? Big-cock, strong cats with Hershey Miniatures dicks," I said, laughing.

She adjusted herself in her seat until her body was facing me before talking. "Demarcus, you must have dated one since you know their dick size. Were you disappointed when you saw his, or were you mad that, even with him taking sports enhancement drugs, his dick was bigger than yours? "

"Stop playing with me, Joyce. Ain't shit about me gay, not even when I'm happy! And if you're curious about my dick, you should have said something. I don't mind whipping it out for you." I let go of the steering wheel and unfastened my pants.

"Stop! Please stop!" she said, laughing. "I see you want us to be back on a first-name basis."

"If I would have pulled this monster out of my pants, we wouldn't have had a choice but to be on a first-name basis."

We made it to Atlanta with an hour and thirty minutes to spare before midnight. She directed me around the city, straight to her mother's house in Stone Mountain.

"I don't know about meeting your family. I don't do—"

"Shut the hell up. You are banned from telling me what you do and don't do for the remainder of the trip. You've already told me about your past, and I have yet to hear you mention any good times. My family is far from what would be called traditional. I bet you two hundred dollars you have the time of your life over here. Just watch out for my aunt Myrtle. She has a thing for cute, younger men, and since she's damn near blind I'm sure she'll find you attractive."

She got out of the car, leaving me with no choice but to follow her to the house. The front porch was covered with people, who all made sure to hug her and introduce themselves to me. One of the guys she was hugging looked over his shoulder and yelled into the house, "Mama, Joyce is here with some nigga!"

"Be nice, Jaylen. His name is Demarcus, and he's just a friend."

"That's the same shit you said about that buff nigga, and the next thing I know you were calling us over to whoop his ass."

Her conversation was cut short as her mother and two other ladies up in age made their way to the front porch. "My baby, I'm glad you made it. I was getting worried about you." Her mother had an islander accent, but I couldn't place the origin of it. It sounded Creole with a touch of Spanish grounding.

"You know I wouldn't miss your New Year's Eve party for nothing in the world, Mama."

As they hugged tightly, I observed that I would have known the woman was her mother without Joyce having to call her Mama because they looked exactly alike. Instead of having brown-tipped dreadlocks, the woman had long silver ones identical in length to Joyce's. Unlike Joyce, her mother had these beautiful light brown eyes and full lips defiantly giving her a one up on her daughter. She was wearing one of those African wraparound dresses, and her hourglass shape said the time was right for Mama. Her curves were perfect, and Mama was brick solid.

"Mama, this is my friend Demarcus from Memphis. Demarcus, this is my mama, Mrs. Pfeifer, but everyone calls her—"

"Mama," Mrs. Pfeifer said, reaching out to hug me. "It's a pleasure to meet you, dear. If Joyce had told me she was bringing her boyfriend, I would have dressed for this special occasion."

"Mama, he is not my boyfriend," Joyce said with irritation.

"Sure, honey, whatever you say. Demarcus, these are my sisters, Amelia and Myrtle. This is Demarcus, Joyce's boy—"

"Mama!" Joyce shouted.

"Joyce's friend from Memphis."

Both ladies pulled me into their bosoms for long, tight hugs, and I didn't want to say anything, but Aunt Myrtle made sure to cuff my ass in the process.

"Your brothers are in the back. Joseph Jr. too," her mama told her, and Joyce shouted through the house, leaving me with the three smiling older women.

"So, Demarcus, how long have you and Joyce been dating?" her aunt Amelia asked, ready to get all the juicy gossip, but there wasn't any to give.

"No, ma'am. We're not dating, just friends."

"Hmm," she said, looking at Joyce's mama.

"Well, if you're crazy enough not to date my niece, I'll give you a chance. I like men who don't need Viagra to get their blood flowing," Myrtle said with a wink.

"Ay, let me holler at you for a second, Damarion," her brother Jaylen said, killing my name.

"It's Demarcus, but what's up?"

Jaylen walked me into the house and took me into the empty den. I could hear the sounds of reggae music bouncing in the backyard.

"Look, playa, I'm going to say this and then leave it alone. You're good with me until you're not good with her. If you're on that more than one woman shit or into putting your hands on one, walk away now. I don't make threats—"

"And I don't take them," I said cutting him off. "If your sister and I ever take it to the next level, I can promise you that you won't have any worries about me. As for right now, we're just friends ringing in the year together. Now where can I get a plate of food like the one you had?"

"Only here. You'll never get any food better than my mama's cooking. She puts it down in the kitchen."

We shook up, and he took me to make myself a plate and grab me a beer. We joined Joyce in the backyard with her brother Joseph Jr.

"JJ, this is Demarcus, Joyce's friend. I already gave his ass the shakedown in the house. He seems cool," Jaylen said while pretending to uppercut me in my stomach as if we were good friends.

JJ stood and gave me the once-over as he reached out his hand for dap. "If you ain't here to get this whooping on the bones table, you got to bounce, homie," JJ said.

"I don't know about taking no whippings, but I don't mind giving out some. Where we at?" I turned and faced Joyce. "Can you put some more duck chili on my plate and wrap it up? I'll eat when we get to your house. I got some ass I need to whip." I kissed her on her cheek before she walked off.

JJ had been in jail before because he hit me with the jailhouse rules that I was all too familiar with. I was killing him on the tables as Joyce danced in a circle with her cousins. The way she was swaying her body had my full attention.

"You like what you see?" JJ asked, lining my eyes up to Joyce's body.

"I do."

"Treat her right. I'm crazy over my baby sister."

"I already know. Jaylen made sure to tell me. But it's not like that between us." My eyes were still locked on her hips. "Not yet anyways. We're just friends."

"You mean, you're one of her clients. The last nigga was too, and we had to beat his ass and put him back in jail. What's the case she's working for you?"

"They're trying to stick me with three murders, and I didn't commit any of them."

"How's it looking? I've been down that route."

Joseph Jr. was shaking his head, and I was sure he was thinking about his own case or, from the looks of him, cases. He had the only yellow skin tone in his family, but it was hard to tell because he was covered in tattoos. He had the normal Atlanta hip-hop swag, and he owned the longest dreads in his family. JJ was also blessed with his mother's light eyes, which made it hard to determine if he was aiming for the pretty boy look or the street thug look. I was stocky, but he had me by fifteen pounds and two or three inches in height.

"Thanks to your sister, it's looking damn good."

I was having a ball chopping it up with Joyce's brothers. Both cats were cool and they weren't on that dumb shit those niggas back in Memphis be on. This was my first time experiencing a family gathering like this, and I loved it. They had me drinking mixed drinks out of pineapples, and joints of weed were being passed around like the shit was legal, and Joyce made sure to stand clear of it. When midnight struck, her mama held a toast.

"To the New Year, new friends, newly rebuilt family bonds, and to new loves. Last year is now in the yesterdays and is only an imprint in our minds as memories. Today is the first day of new beginnings. Take advantage of the opportunity to start over. Look at the person next to you and wish them well as we sip our first drinks of the New Year. I love you all!"

We took our drinks, and the music came back on. Joyce started back dancing, and I started back watching.

"How long are you going to let my sister keep dancing by herself?" JJ took my glass from me. "Go handle that."

I wasn't a dancer, but it was a new year, and I was ready for new things. I walked up behind Joyce and wrapped my hands around her waist. "I guess I owe you two hundred dollars, huh?"

"No worries. I'll include it in my legal fees."

We danced two songs straight, and all eyes were on us. I didn't like the spotlight, but the shit felt right. When the song changed into something faster, I knew that was it for me, until her mother walked up.

"Demarcus, you have two left feet and no rhythm. Let Mama help you out." She took my hands and made me follow her lead. For an older woman, Mrs. Pfeifer still had it. She passed me the joint she was smoking to hit.

"My daughter has experienced heartbreak and she is afraid of the most beautiful gift in this world, which is love. If she gives her heart to you, handle it with care or don't accept it. She deserves the love I shared with her father. Demarcus, my husband would have loved you because you make Joyce smile. Look at my baby girl; she's glowing. In St. Croix, we'd say a woman can only glow when she's pregnant or her soul is happy." She took the joint back and hit it. "I hope she's glowing because of both." She walked off with a smirk.

I wanted to tell her again the situation between Joyce and me, but it was a lost cause. Instead, I yelled behind her, "Yes, ma'am."

***

When we left her mother's house, it around three in the morning, and for the first time I wondered where I would be sleeping. "Did you get me a hotel or am I sleeping with you?"

"No, sir, to both accounts. You will be sleeping in my guest room, and I'll be in my room with my bedroom door double locked."

"Damn! It's like that?"

"Hell yeah! It's like that!"

We pulled up to her three-bedroom house and went inside. The outside was beautiful, but it didn't compare to the inside. She was a little on the messy side. Her kitchen trashcan was overflowing, and her countertops were covered with takeout boxes. Rico had told me while we were in jail that there were two things to look for when a woman invited you to her house, and they were how clean she kept her kitchen and her bathroom. Immediately, I asked if I could go pee. The bathroom was worse than the kitchen, which was a little disappointing. She was close to being the full package minus those dreads, but I couldn't overlook her messiness.

"When's the last time you cleaned this motherfucka up?"

"A few days before Christmas, I think. I mean, that's the last time my maid was here anyways. I sent her home to St. Croix to be with her family for the holidays." She said it without a care in her voice.

"So you can't cook and clean for yourself while she's gone?"

"I could, but why? I pay her to do it. It will stay how it is until she gets back."

Joyce had turned me all the way off.

"Where's my room?"

I didn't bother eating my food. That nasty-ass kitchen had ruined my appetite. I jumped in bed and went to sleep.

Chapter 9

Omar

"Good morning, sir, and welcome to Dee's Communications. My name is Dwayne. How may I help you?"

I walked in just in time to watch Uncle Leroy's junky ass work his magic of bullshitting. "How much is my nephew paying you to sound like a house nigga? You sound damn good, too. Your granddaddy must have been a house nigga, huh? You'd be surprised at what will pass through your genes."

I cleared my voice to get Unc back on track.

"Dwayne, let me be frank with you, son. You can't help me with a motherfucking thing. I'm here to conduct business with my nephew Dee. Where is he?"

Uncle Leroy began dusting off his dirty, torn army green smoker's jacket as if it would give him a more business professional look. But, with those oversized khaki pants he was wearing with a shoelace belt and cut a little below the knees and his once burgundy, now black New Balances, the only business he seemed to be handling were regular transactions with the dope man.

"I'm sorry, sir, but Dee isn't here. He doesn't really come to this location. If you leave your . . . Well, never mind."

"If I leave what? Don't let the cat get your tongue unless that bitch is paying you in ass or cash."

"Excuse me?" This nigga had no idea what Uncle Leroy was talking about and he began eyeing us both, so I spoke up.

"What my business associate was trying to say is, finish your sentence."

Dwayne gave me the same fucked-up look he gave Uncle Leroy. I could tell that he thought our junky asses were a waste of his time. "Oh, okay. I was going to tell you to leave your business card, and I'd make sure to give it to him."

"Business card? Nigga, do it look like I got a business card to leave?" Uncle Leroy snapped. "I don't need a business card. I'm a street hustler, and Dee's my nephew. He told me to come through with twenty of these, and he'd buy them from me at top price!" Unc dug in his pants pockets and pulled out three broken cell phones.

Two were missing the batteries, and the other had a cracked screen.

"I don't have all twenty of them yet, but this is a sample of things to come. I'm his go-to man, and for the right price I can get you anything."

Dwayne could no longer hold his composure and he broke out laughing. "Man, Dee doesn't want these broken-up prepaid phones."

"How are you going to tell me what Dee wants? He told me out his own mouth when I washed his car last week." Uncle stepped to the side and directed his voice at the EMPLOYEES ONLY sign behind Dwayne. "Dee, it's your uncle Leroy. Come from back there. The bird has landed, Dee!"

Unc started screaming for Demarcus to come from the rear where he believed his office to be. Instead, a fat bitch with too much Ampro gel holding down her baby hair came from the back to see what the noise was about.

"Dwayne, what's going on?" she asked, looking from Unc to me.

"These guys are looking for Dee to sell him those cell phones."

She looked at the phones, then back at us. Her eyes set on me for one second too many, so I turned my back to her and rested my elbows on the glass covering the cell phones on display at the counter.

"We don't buy used cell phones, and judging by the condition of these even if we did Dee would fire us for buying them from you." A smile appeared on her oversized mouth to reveal every track on her braces.

"Hold on, bitch! I didn't ask you what you buy and what you don't. I'm doing what my nephew Dee asked of me. Now roll your big ass back to the back and tell my nephew Uncle Leroy is in the building. The pimp is in this bitch!"

The smile on her face quickly disappeared. "First off, you need to stop screaming for Dee. He isn't here. And I'm not your bitch. So take these busted-up cell phones and get out. I don't know what you think this is here, but it ain't that!"

"You gon' talk about a nigga's merchandise in my face like I ain't shit. Where's the manager? I'm not going to put up with this disrespectful shit. A bitch serves his master on all fours, and you done fucked up. When I tell Dee about you disrespecting a pimp, yo' ass getting fired."

"Boy, bye. I am the manager, and you're trespassing."

"How am I trespassing on my nephew's establishment? Ho, you're trespassing."

They went at it and was calling each other every foul word imagined. I let the shit go on until she gave me the information I had come for.

"If you were really Dee's uncle, you'd know he worked out of his barbershop. Now get the fuck out before I have y'all's junky asses sitting in 201!"

"Leroy, grab the cell phones before this bitch calls the police on us. We'll take our business elsewhere," I said, smiling at her.

"Right, niggas is begging me for my services. You just fucked Dee out of some money because you can bet your fat ass he's going to have to pay me for you wasting my time." Unc snatched up the cell phones.

"Whatever, nigga!" she said as we walked to the door.

I thought she was going to let the fact that I called her a bitch slide, but her words cut me like a rusty straight-edge razor that had chopped too much dope. "And don't bring y'all's crackhead asses back! Especially you with your smoked-out Demarcus-looking ass. Ha, Dwayne, that nigga a junky Dee wannabe."

I didn't say shit because the victory was mine. Once I killed the nigga she called boss, the fat bitch would be selling her braces for cash.

"We did that shit, Omar. Now where's my pay?" Uncle Leroy asked, doing the hustle around the bus bench that had an advertisement for Dee's Communications on it with a picture of Dee in a monkey suit.

"Where's his barbershop at?"

He stuck out his filthy black hand and said, "I'll tell you soon as you give me what I need."

"I'm not giving your ass shit until you tell me where it's at!"

"See?" He shook his finger at me. "I told myself not to trust you. You're a snake just like your daddy, but you can't get over on a pimp. I keep my grass cut low for niggas like you. If you don't pay me, my favorite nephew will." Unc was facing me and taking slow, small steps backward. "Do you know how much money Demarcus is going to give me for telling him your ass is still alive and in Memphis plotting on killing him? Nigga, I'll be rich. You ain't never had money like Dee got. Your small fries ain't shit to his homemade mashed potatoes and gravy, nigga."

I pulled out my pistol and hit him across the face with it. He fell over the bus bench with ease. "Then, I should go ahead and kill your ass now, right?" I cocked my gun.

"Hell naw!" Unc said, gripping his face. "Come on, Omar. You know your uncle ain't no snitch. I was just fucking with you. Can you help me get back up?" He had a nervous laugh mixed with a chuckle. "The barbershop is right there in North Memphis off of Jackson and Watkins by the barber college. It's called Chopped Up by Dee.

Put the gun away. We're family. What's money when it comes to helping blood?"

I kept it pointed at him for a while and then placed it back in the small of my back. I knew his loyalty belonged to whichever one of us was keeping him high. "Good looking, Unc. You're right. We family. I gotcha. I'm about to run back to the car and get you straight."

I was gone five minutes, and I could see the anticipation of my return written all over his face. I promised him the other half of the fifty dollar bill and a gram of dog food for a job well done; instead, I handed him a half of one.

"Come on, Omar. This ain't a gram!" he said with disappointment written all over his face.

"I know it's not. Remember, we're family, so I know you ain't shit. Dee paid you to set me up, and for a beer and a few dollars more than what that faggot gave you, you told me his full plan. Ride with me to where you claim the barbershop is, and if it's there I'll give your junky ass the rest."

"Déjà vu," he mumbled.

"What did you say?"

"I was just saying déjà vu. You carry your work in your hand like your mama used to do before she started shooting it up. The rotten apple sitting right under the moldy tree."

"So what'cha trying to say, nigga?"

"I ain't saying shit, Omar. I ain't said a moth-erfucking thing!"

The barbershop sat pretty in that raggedy-ass neighborhood. It had more flashing lights than Las Vegas during tax time. "Chopped Up by Dee, huh?" I said, reading the sign.

"Yeah, but he ain't cutting hair. He snatched up all the best barbers in the city and put them in one place. It's clean as fuck in there, too. Motherfuckas are passing up the club to hang out at the barbershop."

"What about his daddy's strip club?"

"Dee still got it, but some other nigga is run-ning it. On Saturdays nights, some of the hoes who work at the strip club strip off in there," he said, pointing at the barbershop. "That nigga about his paper, nephew. He calls it Strips and Clips Saturdays. You need to cook that beef you got with him and make peace over a meal with your little cousin, and I'm sure he'll help you get back on your feet. Y'all blood, and you want to beef with the most beloved nigga in the city over a bitch he don't even want no more. I thought I taught you the power of the pussy. Good pussy starts wars, and niggas end up dead while the bitch is laid up with the next nigga."

"This shit ain't over that junky bitch Bria. You forgot that that nigga and his daddy sentenced me to death. Ain't no peace until he's dead. Fuck that bitch. I heard she was dead anyways!"

I tried hard to sound believable, but Unc's face proved he didn't buy it. This shit wasn't all about Bria. I had the bitch first but once mine, always mine. I told that bitch 'til death do we part, and I didn't have to seal it with a ring.

"I've been importing and exporting pussy before you or your mama was born. I know a dick sword fight when I see one, Omar, but you ain't gon' win it. Take my advice. Go back to where you came from, and let this shit in Memphis go!"

"Man, shut the fuck up! You want this hit or what?"

He dug in his jacket pocket and pulled out his get-high paraphernalia. "If you stay ready, you ain't got to get ready, you Demarcus wannabe."

I popped my trunk and grabbed the other half of his gram, making sure it was securely wrapped because I didn't want to touch it. "Let me duck off down this street, and you can get you one in before I drop you back off at your basket."

It didn't take long after he filled the syringe with the heated heroin for his eyes to close as he enjoyed his fix. "This shit right here is the next best thing to pussy, nephew."

Those were his last words before I put a bullet through his head. Uncle Leroy was dead on the passenger side of my car with the needle stuck in his arm. Long live the pimp!

I was out a car, and the streets were too busy in the area to try to steal one, so I took a cab. I used the phone in the gas station near Demarcus's barbershop and had the cab pick me up there. I saw a familiar face at the pump, getting gas. I couldn't think of the cat's name, but he used to run with Gutta back in the day. I couldn't risk him seeing me, because if I remembered him I was sure he remembered me. He was driving a new Magnum with the doors that opened like butterfly wings, and he was rocking a large diamond pinky ring. If he was getting money like that, I needed to find a way to take some from him.

I grabbed the bags of ice I'd bought from the gas station and I jumped in the cab. We hit the block in time for me to see the Magnum pull into the barbershop parking lot.

"I should have known you were fucking with Demarcus," I mumbled.

"No, I don't fuck with nobody. You pay me first!" The cab driver thought I was talking to him, but, to prevent a problem, I paid him like he asked me to; and then he closed the bullet-proof window to separate us.

I made it back to the room, and it was hot as hell inside of it. The heater was at ninety degrees and the smell of a dead body was growing louder. I went to handle Sapphire in the tub, but the bathroom door was locked. I tried picking the lock, but it was a no go, so I kicked the door in.

All the ice was melted, and the tub was completely dry. I ran cold water on Sapphire and then poured the motel's shampoo over her before covering her in ice. To me, it looked like a lock of her blond hair was missing, but the patch could have already been missing. I racked my brain, trying to remember; but I couldn't remember shit. I didn't remember turning the heater on, either, but I had fallen asleep high and I ran out the door when I woke up this morning to meet Uncle Leroy. When I was on that dog food, anything was possible.

Opening the door to let the room air out while I ate my almost two-day-old tacos on the balcony, I peeped my surroundings, and everything seemed the same. It was probably me high and tripping, but I would make this my last night in this room.

After I ate, I jumped in the bed early to get a night of good sleep. There was no telling where I'd be sleeping after tonight.

The sun woke me up as it blazed through a crack in the curtains, and I got my ass up to walk and get more ice. The room was paid for, but living with a corpse wasn't sitting right with me, so I grabbed my bags and bounced. I walked until I reached a food spot and I asked to use the phone to call a cab. As I was walking out the door, I ran into a beautiful golden-skinned girl. Our collision almost sent her to the floor, but I grabbed her in the nick of time.

"I'm sorry, baby; I didn't see you come in the door. It's like you magically appeared in front of me."

"You don't look like the type to believe in magic," she said, smiling, obviously overlooking my appearance. "What else do you believe in?" she continued.

"I believe in love at first sight, too."

"Hmm, maybe I'm psychic because I knew you would say that. Have you already eaten? Are you leaving?"

"I didn't eat, but I am leaving. I gotta get cleaned up. My job is done, and I'm ready to get back to me, if you understand."

"This dirty grunge look isn't you?" She sounded disappointed. "I was starting to like what I saw. I'm a huge fan of hygiene, but something about you said that the clothes were dirty but not the person inside of them."

I dug in my pocket and flashed twenty-five one hundred dollar bills at her. The rest of my money was in my bag. "I'm clean, but the job is dirty," I said, putting my money away after she saw it.

"Give me your hand."

I stuck it out, but it was filthy too. She grabbed it and wrote her number in it surrounded by hearts. "I'm starving and I am about to eat, but you should call me sometime. Don't keep me waiting too long," she said, walking into the restaurant.

"Wait. What's your name?"

"I'm . . ."

I could tell she was thinking of a fake name to give me, but I didn't care. "Don't worry about making one up, sweetheart. I'll give you a name when I call you. Mine is Omar, and if you're not busy let's hook up in a few hours, if that's good with you?"

"I'd like that," she said, blushing. "See you soon, Omar."

I had the cab driver take me to the mall. Now that I had plans for the evening, shopping gave me something to do until then. The fact that I didn't have a car had slipped my mind until I realized I had more bags than I could carry and nowhere to put them. I had stolen two cars already and I felt like the third would get me caught up so, against my plan, I had the cab driver take me to a "buy here, pay here" lot. I used to serve the owner dog food for Lord King, and he'd let us borrow cars off his lot from time to time. I didn't have any heroin, but I hoped cash was his other addiction.

"I'm sorry to hear about Lord King but good thing he had Demarcus. I was sure you'd take over with him dead and all."

"I am. I just got to get with Demarcus on it. Have you seen him?"

"Not since my last haircut, but if you're looking for him you should go by his barbershop. He's always there."

I drove off in my Impala with the dealer's plates on it. Candi, which was the name I gave the chick from the restaurant, agreed to meet with me at the hotel inside of the casino in Tunica.

"Damn! I left my ID at the fucking car lot. Can you put the room in your name?"

"We don't need a room; we can have fun without one." I could tell she thought I was trying to have sex with her.

"Baby, I have five thousand dollars' worth of clothes and shoes in the car and another forty thousand dollars in cash in that duffle bag. I need a room to put my shit in the safe."

She was against it, but she gave in after fifteen minutes of me begging. "Give me the money for it and then go over there. I don't let anyone I just met know my government name unless I know for sure they're going to be in my life."

"Okay, Candi, but get the room for me for a week. My apartment should be ready by then."

I gave her the cash, and I knew she didn't believe me, but she went straight to the reservations desk without saying anything. When she came back with the keys, I handed her a hundred dollar bill and told her I was going to put the bags up and get dressed. I told her to try to hit big on the slots until I made it back.

She was sipping on something light at the bar, talking on her phone when I made it back downstairs. I doubted she had played anything. "I'm not, and I'll check in later. I gotta go." She hung up her phone and hurriedly gave me an explanation. "That was my brother; I had to let him know where I was at because he worries about me. Are you ready to play?"

"Yeah, I'm ready."

Something wasn't right about Candi and whatever it was would show its face eventually. I had secrets too, so there wasn't too much I could say. We gambled and drank, but neither one of us won any real money. I had gambled $500 and lost it, and had won $550 back before it was time for us to have dinner.

"So, tell me about yourself, beautiful. Are you from Memphis?"

"There's nothing to tell," she said quickly. 'You seem more interesting than me anyways. Tell me about you. What do you do for a living, and where have you been? You said you were moving back to Memphis, but from where?"

"I really can't discuss my line of work for safety reasons, but I've been in Detroit for the past three years. When my job said they needed to transfer me back home for an assignment, I decided to move back. I love Memphis, and there's no other place like it on this earth."

"You love Memphis? I think that is the first time I've ever heard anyone say that. What is it about Memphis that you love?"

I didn't have to think of an answer. "Memphis gives you an opportunity to own and run your own business with ease. All it takes is a hustle here, and you can be on top quickly."

We ate and then went back to gambling. I tried my luck on the tables, and she headed back to the slots. I was up on the casino $1,700, and they were still feeding me money. When I got to $2,200, I grabbed my chips and cashed out to throw Candi another hundred, but baby girl didn't need it. She had hit a jackpot and had a crowd forming behind her. I tried to get through it, but the casino was in the process of paying her, and security had made everyone step back, but I was in earshot.

"You've won $8,557.62. Congratulations, Sierra, and thank you for playing with us. Can we interest you in a free suite and free admittance to a show?"

She nodded with the biggest and prettiest smile on her face. But it wasn't her smile that caught my attention; it was her name. The name "Sierra" waved a red flag in my head, but I couldn't figure out why. I knew I had never seen her before because nothing about her looked familiar to me, but that name . . . Why did I know that fucking name?

Chapter 10

Demarcus

I woke up to a clean house, a loaded omelet on the kitchen counter, and a note that read:

> *Gone to run errands. There's a new toothbrush waiting for you on the hallway bathroom sink. The spare key is hanging by the front door, so you can do your shopping. The house alarm code is 9229, and the directions to set it are next to it. Be ready to work when I get back.*
> —Joyce

I wasn't familiar with Atlanta, but I remembered the name of the mall I went to during my last trip here, so I put it in my GPS. It was packed, but what else should I have expected with all the New Year's sales going on? It was hard for me to shop because my mind was filled with the highlights from the night before. I had really enjoyed myself with Joyce's family, and I was comfortable. I didn't know her on a dating level, but if we were to take it there, it was good to know I'd be welcomed in by the family.

Macy's and Ralph Lauren got all my money this go-round, and then I went to Walmart and got some pajamas. I wanted to do something nice for Joyce, but she was already getting a lot of my money. I made it back to the house around six, and she wasn't there yet, so I took a shower. I wasn't expecting her to be home when I got out of it and had my towel wrapped around my waist.

"I don't have any ones," I heard her voice say as I passed the kitchen. Joyce had bags full of groceries covering the countertops as she put the food away.

"My fault! I didn't think you'd be home, and I don't strip for ones. I need twenties or better for this monster."

"Boy, get dressed. We have work to do."

I dressed and sat on one of the barstools at her island as she chopped and diced. "You eat seafood, I hope?"

"Damn right, I do."

She handed me a glass of wine as she dropped two whole lobsters into a big, boiling pot.

"Now, tell me everything that happened from Christmas Eve to the days that followed," she said with a tape recorder recording me.

I trusted Joyce but not enough to let her record me. I hit stop on her machine and then took her minute by minute through the days as she fed me parts of our meal with her hand. Now I understood why talking was therapeutic, because it made me remember the surveillance cameras I had on my house. I had cameras pointing everywhere, including at the entrance of the cul-de-sac.

"Can I use your computer?"

"Sure. It's over there," she said with a nod in the direction of the living room.

It only took a few minutes to pull up the footage from Christmas. I watched it without telling her anything. Ten minutes after slapping Bria down my steps, someone exited a car that was parked up the street. He ran right up Bria's driveway and then disappeared. Forty-seven minutes and a few seconds later, he crossed the street back to his car, limping.

"Joyce, you gotta see this shit."

I started the video after the slap because I didn't want Joyce to see that side of me. She gasped when she saw the perpetrator. I sped the video up to after I drove out of the cul-de-sac and, five minutes later, the perp made his exit.

"Move out the way," she said, wiping her hands on her apron. She replayed the video to an hour before the perpetrator made his way up Bria's driveway, and the car was already there. She went back another hour, and it was there too. The car had been sitting there since seven that morning and had only left the street twice. She opened up some software she had on her computer and recorded the video from Christmas Eve until the time the perpetrator had left. She was punching digits in her phone before I could ask what she was doing.

"Can I be transferred to Detective Ryu in homicide please? Thank you. Hello, Detective, this is Joyce Claybrooks, Demarcus Elder's attorney, and I have evidence clearing my client in your investigation that I'm about to submit; but, in return, I need you to clear him in the assault on the victim for cooperating in your investigation." She paused for almost a minute. "Trust me, Mr. Elder just handed you the murderer. All you have to do now is what you're being paid for. I'm sending it via e-mail now, and I would like another one of those pretty letters you type up clearing my client as a suspect when you're done watching the footage. Thanks." She hung up and ran back into the kitchen.

"What do we do now?" I asked.

"I already have tomorrow planned out for you, but Sunday we'll get up early to get my diamond earrings, and then you are free to go back home."

I ate my meal with a smile on my face. In the morning, we went out for breakfast, and then she drove me to downtown Atlanta. She wouldn't say where we were going, but she made me dress comfortably while she was dressed like the lawyer she was, headed to trial.

"We're here," she said, smiling ear to ear.

We were at the Georgia Dome, home of the Atlanta Falcons, but I was sure their season was already over. Colleges sometimes used the Dome to host bowl games, but I didn't recall hearing any announced. The sign at the gate's entrance read: WELCOME TO THE NCAA'S WINTER YOUTH FOOTBALL AND TRAINING CAMP.

"Come on, Demarcus. You're scheduled to speak to the high school seniors in ten minutes," Joyce said, taking off into the arena; but I hadn't moved a bit.

When she realized I wasn't trailing her, she made her way back to me, but I was already being approached by someone I knew.

"Demarcus? Oh, man! It's great to see you again. How are you?" It was Jeff, the guy who had scouted me to play for Alabama. He had his hand extended to me, but all the memories of him sitting on my couch across from me and Mama had me frozen in place. Joyce grabbed my hand and placed it in his, then reached out, and introduced herself to Jeff.

"It's a pleasure to meet you, Jeff, but you two will have to catch up later. Demarcus is set to speak next, and I only have seven minutes to shake off his stage fright. Excuse us."

"Why did you bring me here? This shit ain't cool, Joyce. I'm not even supposed to be around kids, and you bring me to a stadium packed full of them. I'm gone."

"No, you're not going anywhere. You got this, and the NCAA cleared you to speak, and you have the parents' consent. You're doing this, Demarcus. My mother spoke of new beginnings, and this is the start of yours. Now come on."

I still didn't move. "What do you expect me to say to the kids? I got fucked up and raped a bitch and then lost everything within a week's time?"

"Yes!" she snapped. "Well, not in those words, but tell them the truth, including the new letter she wrote after all these years."

Joyce didn't understand where I was coming from. She didn't understand the pain this shit was going to bring back.

"Look, Demarcus, I need you to do this. I'm sure it's going to hurt, but these boys need to hear it. They are now in the shoes you were in, and the guidance you didn't get you have the chance to give to them. Do this for me and those boys, and you can forget about the earrings you owe me. Please."

I didn't get a chance to answer. Members of the NCAA were taking me to the field. I grabbed Joyce's hand and made her join me on the stage. Jeff introduced me to the crowd, which had a hundred boys and their parents in it. He gave them background on me and then read my senior year stats. I had forgotten how good I was until he started naming off all the high school records I had broken as a running back. When Jeff was done, Joyce took the mic.

"So why aren't we watching Demarcus on ESPN on Sundays? Why isn't he wearing any Super Bowl rings? And I know many of you are wondering, if he really was that good, why haven't you heard of him until today? Unfortunately, for Demarcus, he lived for football and never learned about the snakes slithering outside the gridiron. He had his dreams snatched away from him just days before getting his Crimson uniform. Demarcus is here to tell you his story. Listen carefully, young men, and learn from his mistakes. Demarcus?"

I didn't know where to start, so I started with the day Jeff came to the house. I painted a picture of the feelings I felt knowing that I had made it and then I spoke on the painful memories of my eighteenth birthday. I ended with the struggles I'd had finding a job as a sex offender and how I owned a few businesses now. Joyce read the letter Sierra had sent to the courts only a few months ago, and then she opened the floor to questions. When I looked at the audience, the fathers were giving me approving nods, and the mothers were drying up tears. To my surprise, there were a lot of hands up, and Jeff picked who would get to ask their question first.

"My dad said you were supposed to be the next Barry Sanders. Is that true?" a little boy wearing a Michigan jersey asked.

"No, your father is wrong. I was going to be better than Barry Sanders," I said, laughing.

Jeff went through a few other questions from the boys, and then he took one from a mother who was wearing an Arizona College football jersey.

"Did you know your mother was battling cancer before you went to jail? I was diagnosed with breast cancer six weeks ago and with my son, Eric, being the only child, he's thinking of passing on his football scholarship to stay home with me, and I'm against it. Can you please say something to him? He's right here."

"To answer your question first, ma'am, no, I didn't know. My mother was in perfect health as far as I knew. She could have been hiding it so I wouldn't pass up my scholarship to stay home with her, but I'll never know. I wasn't told that she had cancer until I got out of jail, and she was already dead.

"Eric, although this is going to be hard, you got to go build a foundation for your future. Cancer doesn't mean dead, and even if God finds it fit to bring your mother home, you have to be able to take care of yourself when she's gone. I wasn't given the opportunity to build a foundation. I was thrown back into the world, and there were days when I missed the luxuries of jail like having three meals a day and a roof over my head. That's no way for anyone to live. Eric, and whoever else is out there going through something and needs to talk or wants a listening ear, take down my number. Better yet, my e-mail, because that will never change, and I'll reach out to you as soon as I can."

After I gave my e-mail address, the crowd cheered, and I started making my way off the stage. Joyce was holding a pair of cleats, and Jeff was holding a Nike sports bag when I turned around.

"Not so fast, Demarcus. You talked a good game, but the question we all have for you is, do you still got it? Inside this bag, you'll find the practice uniform you never received and a plaque for what you've done today with these boys. The locker room is that way. Suit up and show us what you got in the running back training drills."

How could I turn down an offer like that, especially with the crowd going wild in front of me? Jeff placed an Alabama cap on my head, and I hustled over to the locker room. It was the best day of my life.

When we made it back to the house, I was exhausted. The weed smoke had slowed me down some, but I still had it. I took all my clothes off, except my muscle shirt and boxers, and I fell asleep across the bed.

"Wake up, Demarcus. Three hours is a long enough nap." Joyce had been shaking my leg for what I assumed was a long time because she sounded frustrated.

"I'm up. Come here," I said, pulling her down on top of me. I kissed her on her cheek. "Thank you for today. I needed that. Has anyone ever told you how amazing you are?"

"Yes, I tell myself daily, but thanks for asking," she said with a giggle. I flipped her over onto her back, pinning my weight on her. I stole a peck from her lips.

"Has anyone ever told you how sexy you are and how you're making a nigga want you more and more each day?" I put my lips on hers, and she began kissing me back. Her tongue was in my mouth when I felt her pushing me off her.

"Not with those armpits of yours smelling like that you won't. The truth is I like you. I really do, but I don't accept you how you are. I can't date a drug—"

"I'm done selling drugs."

"I can't date a client."

"As of today, you're terminated from being my attorney."

She laughed. "Most of all, I can't date a man who lives in fear of his past, instead of living for the future."

"You've already been helping me with that, don't you see it?" I said, ready to plead my case.

"And I don't know anything about you like your favorite color or food. I don't even know your allergies."

"Damn! You sound like we're getting married tomorrow. All of that comes in time. I'm asking for us to date and get to know each other, not to jump a broom."

"I'll think about it."

"Well, can I have another kiss while you're thinking?"

"I'll think about that too, but you need to get in the shower and fix that smell. Your dinner is on the counter, getting cold; and, yes, I cooked again. Now, get up, Demarcus. You're killing me."

"Okay, Bria, I'm getting up."

She looked at me like I had lost my mind when I accidently called her Bria, so I jumped off of her. There was no way she was going to give me some pussy now.

We ate in silence, and when I tried to apologize she grabbed her plate and locked herself in her room. I sat in the living room watching TV until two in the morning, and she never came out of her room. I fell asleep on the couch. Later that morning, she woke me up.

"Get up and get dressed. We gotta get you back to Memphis," Joyce said. She was fully dressed.

I looked at my watch and it was a little past 6:30. "Why? What's wrong?" I asked while stretching.

"I don't know. Detective Ryu said they've been looking for you all night and they need you to come in ASAP. I told them I'd find you and bring you in with me."

"I thought I was good on this Bria shit."

"You are, but I don't think this is about that."

She jumped in my Maybach and told me to take her to her Benz and when we made it back, she'd drive us to the station. I wanted to ask her what she thought was going on, but she didn't talk casework in cars.

"What's your favorite color and food?" I asked.

"My favorite color is black, and I love seafood," she answered with a smile.

"Did you always want to be a lawyer?"

"No. I wanted to be a superhero with long, pretty hair and a red and pink cape. That was my dream until I turned eleven and realized that wasn't a real career option. Being a lawyer came second. What about you, Demarcus? Was football your only choice of career?"

"If you laugh at me, I'm pulling this bitch over, and you're walking to Memphis."

"Hold on. Let me get my laughing out now, then." She laughed for thirty seconds and then told me to continue.

"I wanted to be a truck driver. I don't know why, but the thought of constantly traveling and being away from my family gave me comfort. I never thought I'd be as good as I was in football. I never had the ball tossed around to me as a kid, nor did I play football in the streets with the other kids in my neighbor. My mama didn't allow it. The only person who played football in my family who I had known of was my aunt Cat's husband, Big Omar, but even that was before I was born. Okay, it's my turn again. How is it that everyone in your family's last name is Pfeifer, and yours is Claybrooks? Were you married before?"

She shook her head. "I changed my last name before I applied to law school. At the time, I felt like that last name was tied to too much blood and drugs. I've regretted it since the day my new social security card arrived in the mail, but I said if I ever get married, I'm going back to Pfeifer and hyphenating my husband's last name behind it. It's back on me. Do you ever want to get married?" She laughed at the tie to her last answer.

"Are you proposing?" I laughed. "Yes, I want to get married but to the right one. She has to be the full package, and every area she is weak in has to be my strength and vice versa. The next woman to get me on one knee will be my soul mate. I'm not settling for shit less than that. Okay, so you know your mama is thick, right?"

"Damn! You checked my mama out?"

"I couldn't help it. She's bad, and those hips stick out something terrible, but that's because she pushed out three kids. I noticed you have some wide hips on you too. Yeah, I checked you out too. Do you have any kids? If so, how many and where are they at?"

"Do I look like a deadbeat mom to you, Demarcus? I don't have kids, but I do want them, at least two. A pretty little dread-headed girl and boy. Do you have kids? And if so how many and where are they?"

"No kids, but I want them, just not right now. I have to get myself straight first. And speaking futuristically, if those two kids of yours are by me, I can promise you that our daughter will not have dreads. You and your mom make them look good, but my baby girl won't have them."

"I'll keep my comments to myself on that one. There's no need to argue about a future situation. Well, that's good to know. I assumed Bria's two-year-old son was yours given the timeframe."

"What?" I hit the brakes, and Joyce almost hit the windshield.

"I read it in her file that she had a two-year-old son who was in state custody. She was in rehab and parenting classes trying to get him back. You didn't know?"

"Naw, I didn't know."

I turned the music up because our small talk was done. If Bria had a two-year-old son in state custody, there was no doubt in my mind that he was mine. *She's lucky she's already dead, because if I find out the little nigga's mine and she didn't tell me about him, I'd have wanted blood over the lost time.* Maybe that was the serious face-to-face conversation she was begging to have with me. Either way, when she found out she was pregnant, I should have been the first to know.

Chapter 11

Omar

Sierra made me wait to see her sexy ass again. After she hit that jackpot at the casino, she left, promising to return, but she never did. All of a sudden, Tunica had become too far of a trip for her to make, and she was extremely busy. The stranger she acted, the easier it was to remember how I knew her name. I had spent all that time hunting down Demarcus, and he was already looking for me. I knew she had to be working for him because her screensaver on her phone read, Righting my wrongdoings in 2011, and what could be more wrong than sending a man to jail for a rape he didn't commit?

Demarcus thought he was smarter than me and that I wouldn't figure it out, but he was wrong. If he could use Sierra to get to me, I'd use her to get back at him. I made sure to show her the time of her life. We went to the free comedy show the casino had comped her, and then to dinner followed by a night of dancing. I didn't know what Demarcus had said or done to get her to work for him, but whatever he was offering I would double it. I was sure he used the guilt of what she had done to him as leverage and I couldn't touch that, but fear was a motherfucka, and I had enough evil in me to send the devil into hiding.

I waited until we celebrated the New Year with the traditional countdown, and then I convinced her to come back to the suite for a private toast and to grab more gambling money. I handed her a glass of champagne the casino had placed in the suite for us and I made the toast.

"Here's to righting all of our wrongdoings in 2011. Isn't that right, Sierra?"

She dropped her glass on the carpeted floor, and I fired up my doggy treat. That was my new nickname for the loud mixed with dog food blunts I had been rolling more frequently.

"Don't look so shocked. I knew who you were at first sight," I lied. "I was hoping you were really feeling me at first and that you didn't know who I was, but your actions told on you. I've been waiting for you to make a move, but you haven't yet, so tell me what Demarcus's plan is."

"You don't know what you're talking about. I don't know a Demarcus."

I stopped the lies before she hurt her little brain trying to think up more. "Bitch, please. The jig is up. I'm right here in your face telling you that I know Demarcus is using you to get to me, and you're still lying. What I don't understand is why he hasn't attacked. I'm sure you told him I was staying at the hotel. Why hasn't he come to get me yet? I've been waiting."

"You have no idea who you're fucking with, nor do you know what the hell you're talking about!"

I pulled out my gun, pointed it at her, and then walked in her direction, making sure she saw the grin on my face. "That's what I got you for now. You're going to enlighten me on everything, so start talking if you want to live."

She started crying. I knew I was evil but, damn, she didn't even let me torture her first.

"If I help you, he's going to kill me, and, if I don't help you, you're going to kill me. But after listening to what he told me about you, I know if I help you're going to kill me anyways. The way I see it I'm dead either way, so go ahead and do you what you have to do."

"You know what, Sierra? For being a dumb bitch who likes to fuck up people's lives, you're a lot smarter than you look. Yeah, I'm going to kill you. I'm going to kill Demarcus's bitch ass too, but what I need to know right now is, where is he?"

"Why do you think I'm working for Demarcus, Omar? Do you really think that Demarcus would go through all of this just for you? You're already dead to him. So listen well because I'm only going to say this to you once. Kill me now, or I will kill myself. Before you play God and decide which way I'm leaving this earth, please know that Demarcus don't give a fuck about you, and everything that I've been doing wasn't because he told me to. I was setting your ass up for death because I wanted to. I know what you've done to Demarcus, and I know what you've done to other people, too. If you being dead makes it easier for Demarcus and helps me to right my wrong, then fuck your life. But I promise you this: if you stay in this room any longer, the coroner will be carrying us both out in white bags. He's on his way, and I'm not talking about Demarcus."

"Shit. Say no more."

I put the gun to her head and pulled the trigger. She now had a bull's-eye target imbedded in her forehead. I went in her purse and took all the money out of it and then left the room. She still didn't tell me what I needed to know about Demarcus, but I knew my next move would be to visit him.

It was a little past two in the morning, and the casino was still packed with New Year's Eve revelers, but I didn't want to risk the chance of walking through the main exit. I took the stairs back down to the first floor and used the fire exit to leave. The alarm sounded, but once I closed the door it went off.

I found an old dirt road somewhere between Memphis, Tennessee, and Tunica, Mississippi, and I pulled into the driveway of an abandoned house. I drove into the backyard and parked the car behind the house, so I couldn't be seen from the street. I'd get me some sleep today, but when the sun rose again tomorrow, it was on.

I sat at the barbershop and waited for it to open at eight that morning. Three guys in different cars pulled up all at the same time but they didn't get out of them. This was it. I could feel it, but this wasn't the way I wanted to die. I started my car up, put it in reverse, and hit the gas as hard as I could, when another car pulled in, blocking my exit. I grabbed my gun from the seat next to me and took it off safety. If I was going out, I was going to take as many niggas as possible with me. It was the Magnum I'd seen at the gas station the other night, but a different driver got out of it and flagged me down. I put my gun on my lap and cracked my window.

"Are you trying to get your hair cut? Sorry I'm late. I'm opening up right now. Pull back up."

He ran to the door and unlocked it, and then the guys got out of their cars with their cutting tools and aprons on. Those doggy treats had me paranoid and the talk I'd had with Sierra last night hadn't made it any better. I pulled back up, parked, and walked in. The guy who came to my car met me at the door.

"Sorry about that, man. I had a long night, and the liquor wouldn't let me go. I'm Spank, one of the managers here."

"No problem. I'm just trying to get my day started with a fresh cut, you got me?"

"Naw, I don't cut, but Cellous will get you straight. Just sit in the first chair, and he'll get you in a minute."

"All right."

I sat in the seat, and in a few minutes Cellous came from the back, buttoning up his uniform shirt. I told him what I wanted, and he went to work on me.

"Ay, Spank, have you heard from that nigga Dee? He's been off the radar for a minute now," Cellous asked.

"You know how that nigga Dee do. He's probably somewhere lying up, in love," Spank said, laughing. "Why? What's up, Cellous?"

"I heard from Bo's mama that they found that nigga's uncle dead somewhere around here. I just wanted to pay my respects. I'm going to miss his junky ass coming in here, trying to sell us bullshit."

"Damn! For real? He didn't tell me that. Let me call the nigga and see what's up." He pulled out his phone, but I never heard him have a conversation. After a few minutes, he pulled out his phone again.

"Dee just texted and said for me to meet him at his house in hour. I'll see what's up then. That nigga has had a lot of death hit him all at once. That might be why he's staying low. I know I would."

"Yeah, death will send you into hiding. I've seen it happen too many times," I chimed in. Then, a domino reaction filled the room. Everybody had their two cents to put in.

"Yeah, Bo's mama said he got shot in his head. I told that nigga about stealing people's shit and trying to sell it back to them. Y'all remember that time he took my jacket out of my car and walked back in here trying to sell it like I didn't know it was mine?" Cellous said, shaking his head.

"Hell yeah! I remember that," Spank said, damn near in tears from laughing. "That nigga tried to sell it to me for $2.75 and the rest of my French fries. Damn, I feel for my nigga Dee."

I don't know who said what but, one way or another, they started talking about how much I looked like Demarcus.

"Have you ever seen Demarcus?" Spank asked me.

"Only on the commercials, but bitches stop me all the time thinking I'm him," I said, laughing.

"That's free pussy, ain't it, Spank?" Cellous chimed in.

"Hell yeah, it is. If you didn't have that fucked-up Detroit accent, I'd say y'all was brothers. Shit, y'all might be; the nigga don't know who his daddy is," Spank said, laughing.

"I thought LK was that nigga's daddy," another voice from the other side of the room said.

"Hell naw. Rico's bitch works out there at Methodist Regional North. She said Demarcus tried to give that nigga blood to keep him alive, but the DNA test said they were not related. Don't repeat that shit, y'all. You know he fucked up in the head over it, but some way he still ended up getting LK's shit. He left Demarcus with all his shit, except what the narcotics unit had confiscated."

"Damn! What they take?" Cellous asked.

Spank started naming all types of shit that I didn't even know Lord King owned, and I had worked for him for over ten years. That's what

I loved about the barbershop, though. You always have one bitch nigga in it ready to tell it all. If I'd have come here first, Uncle Leroy would still be alive. I sat back on quiet, getting an earful of the information Spank was letting come out of his mouth. If he was Demarcus's right-hand man, he needed to be fired, but since he was running his mouth I wanted to see what else he knew.

"Ay, Spank, whatever happened to that nigga's cousin Omar? I went to school with him back in the day. That nigga owes me like three hundred dollars on some bad work he gave me. I've been looking for him for a minute now," I said.

"You can chalk that shit up as a loss now, play-boy. Omar's been dead almost three years now. He fucked over LK and got turned into fish food. If you're looking for him, check the Mississippi River first."

"Damn," was all I managed to say.

The conversation moved to sports and then right back to Demarcus. "And you owe me fifty dollars, Mike. Demarcus ain't attending ol' girl's funeral. They tried to pin the murder on him. The nigga Demarcus caught her fucking off with told the police Demarcus had hit her a few hours before she died. I told that nigga to leave that bitch alone."

"I don't owe you shit," Mike said while cleaning up his workstation. "He's not going to the funeral because her folks ain't having one. She's getting burned in a box. I ran into her uncle at the post office, and he said that was her wish. She wants her ashes spread somewhere in Florida, so they're going down there when it warms."

"The Keys," I said out loud and shouldn't have. "I'm guessing the Keys; it's real nice down there. If it were me, that's where I'd want to be spread."

Bria and I had talked about death in more detail than we ever discussed life. I knew her plan like the back of my hand. She didn't care what time of year she died, she wanted her service to be held in the heart of the summer. She didn't have plans. They was more like demands. Everyone who attended must be in white with gold accessories. The women who attended needed to have all-white umbrellas that were trimmed in white lace, and the men needed to wear all-white golf hats. She didn't care the age nor the size of the guest. If they planned on attending, those were the two mandatory requirements. She wanted all instrumental music that you step to playing, and she wanted her husband and kids to do the honors of pouring her into the water.

"So the bitch wants to be fed to the fish for real?" Spank asked Mike.

"I guess so," he said.

Cellous spun me around, placing me in front of the mirror, and I jumped. I was Demarcus's twin now. All I needed was a monkey suit, like the one he wore in his commercials, and to gain my weight back. I needed to ease up on the doggy treats, too, because it was showing. It looked like my skeleton was pushing through the flesh, and I couldn't have that.

"You straight?" Cellous asked.

"I'm good, just didn't realize how fine I was. What do I owe you for hooking me up?"

"Twenty-five dollars."

I paid him and pulled off. I parked at the gas station, waiting for Spank to leave, so I could follow him to Demarcus's house, and he led me right there. When he pulled into the driveway, I kept going down the street and parked a block down and waited. I sat out there two hours, but Demarcus never pulled up. I got out of the car and headed down the street. Spank wasn't in his car anymore, which meant he had a key, and I wanted it.

"Who is it?" Spank said, opening the door.

I had my gun pointed at him. "It's the last face you'll ever see. Get your bitch ass back in the house, nigga."

I got him in the house and sat him down on one of the dining room chairs. "You thought I was dead, huh?"

"Nigga, I don't even know who you are. You came to the barbershop for a cut, and I thought you were righteous, but I see you're on that bull-shit too," he said, trying to play the tough role.

"You didn't think I was righteous. You called me fish food remember? It's Omar, nigga. Surprise!"

"Naw, the surprise will be on you when Dee gets here."

"It might, but you won't live to see it!"

"Lord King said those ho-ass niggas probably cut a deal with you. That's why they're both dead now!"

"Shut up, bitch. You talk too damn much. Get up!" I cocked my pistol on him.

"Fuck you. I'm not going anywhere!"

"Cool!"

I emptied every round I had left in my gun into him and then I took his from his holster. This nigga only had two bullets in his gun, and I was all out. I started searching the house for a gun, but all I kept finding was money. Demarcus had money stashed in shoeboxes, under every mattress in the house, and in all of his dresser drawers, but he didn't have one gun in this bitch.

I packed all the money I found into a duffel bag he had in his closet and I set it on the bed. I needed bullets bad. I went back into the dining room and took Spank's phone.

I sent Demarcus a text. Where you at?

Five minutes later, he texted back. Change of plans. I'll hit you up tomorrow with the info.

Are you still coming through?

He didn't text back, but that didn't mean shit to me. I wasn't going anywhere until I saw him, even if that meant moving into this bitch.

I snatched the shower curtain off the bar and put Spank's body on top of it. I dragged it back to the bathroom, threw him in the tub, and locked the door. I found some cleaning supplies underneath the kitchen sink and cleaned up the blood that had splattered on the walls and floors. Once shit was back like it was, I grabbed Spank's keys and jumped in his car. I was going to get me some bullets one way or another.

Chapter 12

Demarcus

We made it to Memphis around 1:00 p.m. and decided to go straight to the station. I had told Spank to meet me at the house almost two hours ago, but traffic killed those plans. We were taken straight to the interrogation room when we arrived. I prepared myself for Detectives Ryu and Rawlings's Partner of the Year act, but I wasn't ready for what I got instead.

"Mr. Elder, this is Sergeant Davis and Lieutenant Parks. They will be sitting in with us today."

"What's going on?" Joyce asked, her face flushed with concern.

Detective Ryu stepped up to the table and took a seat before talking. "We have reason to believe that Mr. Elder is in danger."

"How?" Joyce and I said in unison.

"The video you sent us was very valuable to our case but not just this one." Detective Ryu pulled out printed pictures of the video we sent. "Do you see the car in the picture? It turned up at another crime scene, but this time the driver was gone, and the victim was left inside of it."

He handed me a picture, and there was Uncle Leroy dead as a doornail. A tear dropped from my eye, but I was okay. Uncle Leroy's death was the only one I had prepared myself for. With all the drugs he was using and shit he was stealing from people, I knew he wasn't long for this world, but that didn't mean it still didn't hurt.

"Do you know Courtney Schwartz?" Sergeant Davis asked.

"No, who's that?"

"She's another murder victim. We found the killer's fingerprints at the crime scene. Here, take a look at her and see if anything comes to mind."

Ryu handed me a mug shot of a white girl I had never seen in my life. "I told you. I don't know her."

"I'm sorry, fellas, but what makes you think my client is in danger? That's the part that we are interested in. Spare us pictures of dead women my client doesn't know."

Rawlings stepped up. "Okay. Well, here's a name your client does know. Our last victim tied to this same killer is Sierra. I'm sure that rings a bell for both of you. Sierra was found with a single bullet through the head at a casino in Tunica. We were able to get this clear shot of the killer." Rawlings placed a picture of Omar on the table.

"Demarcus? That's impossible. He was in Atlanta speaking at a NCAA event," Joyce said with too much attitude in her voice.

"That's not me. That's Omar."

"But I thought you said he was dead."

Joyce knew she had fucked up by saying that, and all the officers' ears shot to the ceiling like bloodhounds'.

"Dead? Where did you get that information from, Ms. Claybrooks? Your client told us in a previous interrogation that Omar had gone missing."

Rawlings wasn't wasting any time, but I had her back. "Omar is dead. That's Omar Jr. you're looking at, Joyce."

"Stop with all the lies, Mr. Elder. I've already heard enough of them from you in the short time I've been in this room." Sergeant Davis was pissed, and his white skin had turned red. "I'm going to ask you some questions, and then I'll tell you the answers. Who was Keith Willis to you?"

"He was a man I thought was my father, but y'all told me differently."

"Lie," Sergeant Davis shouted at me. "He was a drug lord who went by the name Lord King who Omar, LP, and Killa worked for. You grew up not knowing who your father was until he confessed not long ago. Next question: what happened to Omar? And don't give me that lame 'missing' excuse."

"Omar got into it bad with Lord King, and he disappeared."

"There goes another lie. Omar got into it bad with you, and Lord King had him killed, but he managed to get away; or so that's the story your friend Rico gave us. Final question: why would Omar want you dead?"

"Because he thinks what you think: that I let Lord King sentence him to death."

"Now we're getting somewhere," Sergeant Davis said, taking a seat across from me, next to Detective Ryu.

"Demarcus, as your lawyer, I have to advise you to be careful what you say."

"Are you suggesting that he lie to us, Ms. Claybrooks?" Ryu said.

"No. I'm suggesting that he doesn't incriminate himself without you first presenting him some kind of deal for doing so."

I was tired of listening to them go back and forth because it was getting us nowhere. "Look, this is what I know. Omar stole the house I inherited from my mother by acting like me while I was in jail. When I came to take it back, he wanted to kill me. Omar did work for Lord King back in the day, and with Lord King thinking he was my father, he wasn't about to sit back and let Omar kill his only child, so he had LP and Killa kill him. Before Lord King was killed, he assumed Killa had made a deal with Omar to spare his life for money, which turned out to be true, or Omar wouldn't be killing people left and right trying to get to me now. The only reason Omar wants me dead is because of the hit Lord King put over his head because of our beef."

"Come on, Demarcus. you can do a little better than that," Rawlings said, hitting the table out of frustration.

"Fuck you mean? That's it. End of story."

"No, it's not." Lieutenant Parks had finally opened his mouth. "Omar has a lot of reasons to want you dead, and you know it. Who is L'Amir?"

"Who? I don't know a L'Amir."

"You've heard my client's side of things. How about you all start sharing the information you have? Maybe if we all work together we can fill in the gaps of the story," Joyce shouted.

Lieutenant Parks made his way to the table and took a seat and so did Rawlings. "L'Amir is the brother of Symphony. She's a dead girl from Detroit whose car Omar stole and drove to Kentucky. The detectives up North found two bodies shot up and burned to death in what looks like a planned apartment explosion that Omar caused. The other body belonged to a drug lord named Franco. He is the son of the founder of the Doggy Cartel, which is run by Haitians, and is the largest heroin distributor on the Eastern and Northern halves of our country."

Joyce opened up her legal pad and began taking notes as Lieutenant Parks continued, "A 911 dispatcher received a call informing them of a large drug supply that was supposedly owned by L'Amir and information that Franco had confessed that the Doggy Cartel had committed the murders of Omar's parents. A few days after that, a young lady reported her car had been stolen in Kentucky by a guy named Omar Brown who told her he was from Memphis. Her car was found in the same parking lot that the one in the picture was stolen from. The car in the picture was at both Bria's and, of course, Leroy's crime scenes and was covered in Omar's prints. We found Courtney's body thanks to an anonymous tip that named Omar as her killer, and the prints and semen taken from the crime scene matched what we got from Bria."

"But you still haven't said who this L'Amir guy is," Joyce said.

"L'Amir is a known employee of Franco's. He got arrested while he was with Omar for driving on a restricted license and a parole violation. Omar tried to get L'Amir more time by saying the drugs were his, but it didn't work. Another person took ownership of them, clearing L'Amir. When you are on the Doggy Cartel's payroll, you don't stay in jail long, and we don't believe Omar knew that. We found Sierra's cell phone at the crime scene filled with death threats. The texts told her that if she wanted to save her and her mother's lives, she needed to do right by Demarcus by helping you to get rid of Omar. L'Amir tried to trick her into thinking you wanted her to do it, but she was smarter than that and told it to L'Amir in a phone call she recorded. She volunteered to help L'Amir get Omar if that meant Omar's death would make your life easier, but Omar got to her first," Lieutenant Parks said, leaving the table and taking his spot back by the wall.

"So do you think this L'Amir guy is after Demarcus, too?" Joyce asked.

"No, we think he's on a manhunt for Omar. He killed L'Amir's sister, his boss, and tried to put him and the rest of the Doggy Cartel away for a long time. L'Amir has a lot of reasons to go after Omar, but we thought he might have reached out to Demarcus for help since Sierra had Demarcus's number in her call log," Rawlings said.

"She called me saying somebody had threatened her to help me, but I hung up on her." My throat was dry, and my head was throbbing, but I needed answers.

"Come on now, Ryu. You're a highly decorated detective. I've been in your office. There are plaques and medals hanging everywhere. There's something you're not telling us." Joyce was out of her chair and walking around the room like she was the detective.

"There's nothing of importance left to tell about this case, besides that we are putting Demarcus in our witness protection program until Omar is captured."

"No, the fuck you're not. I'm not hiding from my cousin. If he wants me, let him come get me. I got something for his bitch ass," I yelled.

"You want to switch places with him? Is that what you're saying? You want to become the murderer now?" Rawlings asked me.

"I have a room full of cops telling me that this man wants me dead. If I kill him first, it's self-defense."

"That's not how that works, Demarcus. I mean, Mr. Elder," Joyce said, trying to maintain professionalism.

"She's right, Demarcus. He would have to attempt to kill you first, and I don't think you will walk away alive if Omar tried to kill you," Rawlings continued.

"Well, I'm not going into a witness protection program, so what else do you have in mind?"

"What if I took him to Atlanta with me?" Joyce offered.

"When Omar can't get to him, he'll come looking for you for answers. You're his lawyer."

"But he doesn't know that, Rawlings," Joyce rebutted.

"You don't know what he already knows. Don't forget about Jacob. He gave you the job, and he was once Lord King's and Omar's attorney. He'll tell it all when he has a gun pointed at his head," Ryu responded.

"What about my mother's house? She'll accept Demarcus."

The room fell silent, and both the lieutenant and sergeant walked out. A few seconds later, Ryu and Rawlings followed their lead.

"I can't let you put your family in danger, but I'm not going into a protection program. I'm not running from Omar ever again. I've run from him all of my life. If that nigga wants a faceoff, then that's exactly what he will get."

Detective Rawlings walked back in the room by himself. Joyce leaned over and whispered in my ear, "Here comes the bullshit. They sent him back in here alone for a chat, black man to black man, but they're watching us through the glass."

"What did you decide, Demarcus? I really feel the protective services we're offering you are your best option. That's what I'd do if I were in your shoes," Rawlings said, retaking his seat.

"I'm not going into witness protection, but if it's cool with Ms. Claybrooks's mom, I'll go out there for a while."

"Why? Do you want to end up dead, Demarcus? You have so much to live for. Look at your businesses. They are flourishing, man. It's hard for a young black man in Memphis to get ahead legally, and you're doing it. I've done my research, and you're legit. You started your businesses with your inheritance money. There isn't a dime of drug money tied to them. Why lose it all?"

There went the black card Joyce knew he would pull.

"Honestly, Rawlings, black man to black man, I don't have shit to live for. Omar is my last living blood relative, and he wants me dead. I don't have shit but me in this world. Whether it's death or I end up getting sentenced to life, I'm losing either way."

Rawlings made eye contact with Joyce as he spoke with me. "What if I told you that you do have a something to live for? You have a two-year-old, heroin-addicted son who needs you to come get him out the system. He needs his father. Don't let him go through what you went through and not know who his father is. Look at how long it took you to find out who your dad was."

"The little nigga is mine, huh?" What a fucked-up way to find out I had a son. "Damn, Rawlings. You're a heartless motherfucka."

He stood, pissed like I had given him the bad news. The door flew open as Ryu and the sergeant walked in.

"Cut the shit, Demarcus. All we've been doing is trying to help you. If I was a heartless mother-fucka, I would have told you who your biological father is. Now that's being heartless."

Ryu was trying to remove his partner from the room, but he had information that I wanted.

"Who is he, since you're running your mouth about everything else?"

Rawlings was out of the room, and I was left with Sergeant Davis and his many apologies.

"Who's my daddy, Sergeant Davis? If he knows who my pops is, I'm sure you know too."

Sergeant Davis didn't say shit, but Joyce did. "It's Omar, Demarcus. You and Omar have the same father. He's your brother. Isn't he, sergeant? That bogus line of questioning was to see if Demarcus knew, wasn't it?"

I looked at them both, not knowing what to say. "Yes, Ms. Claybrooks, they are brothers."

"Get the fuck out of here!" I yelled.

"No, Mr. Elder, it's true, but we only found this information out this morning. We found a divorce petition your aunt filed with the courts wanting to terminate her marriage due to adultery. Her husband had an affair with your mother and that affair produced a child. Nothing ever came of it—"

"Hell naw. Show me the papers. Big Omar isn't my father. My mama hated that nigga. Show me a fucking blood test or something. Omar isn't my brother. Joyce, you better make them show me something now. Right fucking now."

Sergeant Davis left the room, and I went off on Joyce like she had said the bogus shit. When I broke down in tears, she was crying right along with me.

"Stop crying," I said to Joyce as I wiped the last tears out of my eyes. "If he comes back in here with proof, Omar's ass is as dead as our daddy."

Chapter 13

Omar

I sat in the car close to five minutes, trying to think of where I could buy the bullets from, but everywhere that came to mind would require me to use my identification. My body count was high, and I wasn't going to risk the chance of going to jail and not killing Demarcus because I was thirsty for bullets. I'd seen him fight, and I knew what he was working with, but my hands were faster. A gun wasn't the only way to off somebody; it was just the easiest method.

I walked back in the house and thought about hitting up my Mexican connect but I didn't want to risk the chance of getting pulled over in Spank's Magnum. He was riding with illegal tint on his windows, and the drive-out tag in the back window had expired almost two weeks ago. I didn't want to keep taking chances in the car I had because I had promised to turn it in yesterday, and if I didn't show up with a fix for him, or money, I knew he'd report it stolen.

I was hungry and hadn't eaten in almost two days. The dog food wouldn't allow me to have an appetite, even when I knew I should be eating, and even my supply of it was almost gone. I looked in the refrigerator and found me some ham and cheese. This nigga didn't have any mayo. All he had was some ketchup and a jar of honey mustard. I made me a couple of ketchup sandwiches and grabbed the open beer he had in the refrigerator. I didn't know when Demarcus would return home, but I made his house mine anyways.

I went in the bedroom and relaxed on his bed with the television on. I caught the last twenty minutes or so of *Friday* and then *How High* came on. I only had a half of a piece of my doggy treat, and although I said I was going to quit, I couldn't watch the movie without wanting to smoke it.

When that went off, I went through Demarcus's drawers and found me a pair of Kenneth Cole pajamas and I jumped in the shower that was in his room. The water felt good hitting my still healing body, but I was too high, and the steam was fucking with my head. I started getting dizzy and, before I could do something about it, I was lying on the shower's floor, bleeding from my head.

I must have fainted because I didn't remember hitting the floor. I turned the shower off and got out. While stepping on my pile of dirty clothes, I thought I heard the front door close, so I ran out of the bathroom and to the hallway naked. I didn't see anything or anyone, but I had to make sure. I walked to the front door, and it was unlocked. I couldn't remember if I had left it like that, but I was pretty sure I would have remembered to lock it behind me. I did a quick check of every room in the house, but I didn't see anyone.

I went back to the bathroom to bandage up my head with my dry towel and I threw my pajamas on. I had to give it to Demarcus, the little nigga had taste, because the pajamas felt like butter against my skin. I found a pair of house slippers under the bed, and putting those on made me feel like a king in his kingdom. I didn't know how I was going to pull it off, but I needed this house, especially the California king bed he had. It felt like I was lying on a stack of feathers and, even though I didn't try to, I fucked around and fell asleep.

Checking the clock on his DVD player, I realized I was knocked out for close to two hours,

and now that I was awake I was stuck with
boredom to keep me company. Demarcus must
have been an undercover faggot because he had
more chick flicks in his DVD collection than
any man should own. I couldn't find shit that I
wanted to watch until I ran across a burned DVD
that wasn't labeled. It only took a few seconds
of watching it to know that it was a homemade
flick of him and Bria. The first few minutes
of watching it pissed me off. Bria had been
giving Demarcus the same treatment she used
to give me and saying some of the same shit. I
guess it was the bitch's routine and, knowing
Demarcus's green ass, he probably thought he
was the first nigga she treated that way.

Bria was sucking the life out of the Demarcus
and he had his ugly-ass toes balled up like a
fist. I wondered who they had trusted as the
cameraman. When I had my boy record us, she
played the shy role, but with this nigga she was
triple X-rated. And then Demarcus got up and
readjusted the camera to the bed. He was killing
her shit, and she was screaming bloody murder.
Listening to her moans of pain mixed with
pleasure made me pull out my meat and stroke
it. I wanted some pussy bad, but I knew how to
handle it myself.

I turned the volume up as high as I could, so I could hear Bria's moans as I walked to the hallway bathroom and picked the lock with my thumbnail. Spank's eyes were still open, and it gave the impression that he was looking at me. I grabbed the lotion from the medicine cabinet and heated it with my hands, leaving the bathroom hurriedly. I covered my meat with it all the way back to the bedroom and lay on the bed, killing my hand. I closed my eyes and pretended it was Bria was riding me instead of my bitch-ass cousin, and that was when I heard the clip get snapped into the gun.

"You're a nasty motherfucka, Omar. You know that, don't you?"

I continued to beat my meat. If L'Amir was going to kill me, I was going to get a nut in first.

"You gon' keep stroking your shit like a nigga ain't standing here? As a matter of fact, go ahead and get your nut. It's the last one you'll ever get."

"What's up with you, L? When did you touch down?" I asked, while continually stroking with my eyes on Bria's bouncing titties.

"I'm not about to have a conversation with you while you're doing that shit. Hurry the fuck up, nigga. I don't have all day."

"Shit. You invited yourself to this party. You're on my time."

"Your time is up, and you need to shut up before you fuck up me granting you this last wish."

I ignored him. "How's your sister doing?" I exploded at the sound of me saying her name. It immediately made me remember the warmth she held in between her big-ass thighs.

"Symphony has seen better days, but I think you already know that."

"No, what's going on with her? She put me out over Franco. I found out they was fucking behind my back. When I left you at the jailhouse and made it back home, that nigga was laid up with her in my bed."

I had to try to lie. Nobody knew the real truth, but me, Franco, and Symphony, and out of the three of us I was the only one who still had a heartbeat.

L'Amir threw a towel at me to clean myself up with before he continued talking. "Is that what happened? Well, the funny thing about that story is I called my sister from jail to tell her that Franco was coming through. She told me he had already been by, and he was mad that he hadn't heard from you. She said she had been sick, and Franco knew what was wrong with her. He told her you had been feeding her dog food, and she was addicted to the shit and having withdrawals. I tried to call Franco back after talking to her but couldn't get through. I called his sister, the queen of the cartel—"

"His sister? What the fuck are you talking about? He ran the Doggy Cartel after his pops got toe-tagged," I corrected him.

"Nigga, shut the fuck up. You sound dumb. You don't know shit because no one trusted you enough to tell you shit. Like I was saying, I called his sister to see what was up, and you know what she told me? She told me Franco and my sister blew up in y'all's apartment, and her goons said you were nowhere to be found. Your car was there. The van was there, but my sister's shit was missing."

"Damn. For real? Is that what you heard? Yeah, Symphony's ass was with Franco, and I got pissed off and jumped in her car. I thought about going back and trying to make the shit work, but then I was like, 'Fuck it,' and came on back home to Memphis."

"Okay, so you know about my refrigerator truck being raided?"

"Hell no, how did they found out about that? Your truck has been sitting in the same spot in front of the store for almost three years. Somebody in the cartel must have snitched on you."

"Yeah, somebody on the inside did try to snitch on me, but when you're in the cartel they already have somebody ready to take the blame when shit goes south, you feel me?"

"So you got off? That's cool. Did you find out who told on you?"

"Yes, sir. I'm looking at the ho-ass nigga right now."

I pulled my pants up and jumped up off the bed. "Who the fuck do you think you are breaking into my people's house and accusing me of some bullshit like that? Nigga, there ain't a snitch bone in my body. You better take your ass on. You're trying to put it on me because I came back to Memphis."

"You know how to lie your ass off, Omar, but you're not good at it. Did you think they could pin that truck on me without telling me how they found out about it? They had to give my lawyer a copy of the transcript from your 911 call. You snitched on me, Franco, and that nigga's folks."

I took a few steps closer to him. My gun was under the pillow on the bed, but I knew I only had two bullets left in it. I only had a few seconds to come up with something, and I didn't know what I was going to do, but the longer I kept the nigga talking, the longer I stayed alive.

"Nigga, I've never dialed 911 in my life and especially not for some bullshit like that. Is that why you call yourself rolling up on me in Memphis because of this bullshit you made up in your head? You don't even have proof that it was me on the motherfucking phone."

"You're right. I didn't have proof, but you fucked up when you said the shit about your parents. You made it too easy to look up the Mississippi River murder of 1995. Those naked motherfuckers left behind a son to be raised by his aunt. I found out who the aunt was from a newspaper article about a pimping preacher and found out she was dead but not her son."

"Demarcus hooked you up with that bitch Sierra?"

"No, I hooked me up with her, and you killed her. I was just starting to feel her ass, too."

"I didn't know she was working for you, if that makes you feel better. I killed the ho for what she did to my cousin."

"You got me doing too much rappin' and not enough cappin'. Sit your bitch ass down on the bed, youngster. I should have killed you back when we were on the Greyhound."

I did as I was told, and then we both heard the front door open. When L'Amir looked over his shoulder and into the hallway, I grabbed my gun from under the pillows. I put my last two bullets in him through the pillow. When his ass hit the ground, I snatched the gun out of his hands and met Demarcus somewhere in between the living room and the front door.

"Just the man I've been waiting for. What's up, Demarcus?"

I had the gun in my hand, and this nigga was unarmed, but that didn't stop him from running at me at high speed. Before I could point the gun at him, he tackled me to the floor. I guess this nigga thought he was still playing football.

Chapter 14

Demarcus

Detective Ryu had given me the documentation that I needed to confirm we were brothers. Just like that, my only cousin became my only brother. The shit made my stomach flip. My mama wasn't shit for fucking her baby sister's husband. There wasn't a good enough excuse in any book that would give her a pass for crossing those boundaries. Omar was older than me, and Aunt Cat had been married to Big Omar before his junior was ever born. My mama was foul for this one. I don't know if he paid her for the pussy, raped her, or if she outright gave it up, but, as soon as she found out that she was pregnant by her sister's husband, she should have aborted me, instead of fucking my life up.

Now I knew why my aunt Cat hated me so much. I was the love child she had to constantly look at. I was a reminder of not only her husband stepping out on her, but the fact that he had cheated on her with her sister. I could understand why she ran to dog food. It probably helped her ease the pain some. For years, I thought my aunt was below my mama when, in all actuality, Mama was as low as it gets. The prostituting she was doing didn't compare to what she had done to her sister. That was what she should have been embarrassed about.

All my life I had to hear people rant on how much Omar and I looked alike, and in that same moment I'd hear people say that he was the dark-skinned version of his daddy. I guess we both were. He took after the drug-dealing side of our father and inherited his football talents. The shit was starting to add up, and the reality of it was heartbreaking.

Mama hated that I loved football and she had even tried to stop me from playing. She wanted me to get into basketball, but I craved the contact. My mind replayed the conversation between Uncle Leroy and my mama on the last day I had seen Aunt Cat alive. He had said, "While you sitting over there hoping the Lord forgave me, you better pray that all that pussy you was given them pimps was forgiven too. Who's Dee's daddy anyway since you want to bring up the past? You sho'nuff didn't get pregnant by the Lord! You love to talk about other people's mistakes, but don't forget she ain't the only one I took to the stroll in this family. She's just the only ho in this family who said no!" It all made sense now.

It took Detective Rawlings calming his ass down and thinking like a detective before all the other officers agreed on me going to Atlanta. They told Joyce to leave the police station and hit the interstate straight back to Georgia, but I was driving and needed to get my shit first. We didn't know that Detectives Rawlings and Ryu had been following us until I pulled up at my house.

"This doesn't look like the interstate to me, Demarcus," Detective Rawlings said from the driver's seat.

"I have to grab me some clothes and my papers before I get low."

He got out of his car and slammed the door. Ryu followed his lead. "Okay. That's fine, but we're going in with you," Detective Ryu said. "Whose car is this?"

"It belongs to one of my homeboys. He has a spare key to my house. He must be in there."

"Then, we're coming in."

"Look, fellas. You both have already violated my client's rights by following him against his will. Let him go in the house and grab his clothes by himself. That's the least you can do after all of the stuff you told him today. Give Demarcus a break. Damn." Joyce was beyond pissed.

The detectives looked from one to the other, and then Rawlings said, "You have five minutes, not a second more, and then we're coming in there behind you, welcomed or not."

Joyce walked me up the driveway, but I sent her to get her car out of my garage and place mine back in it. My Maybach was known, and I wouldn't give Omar the satisfaction of catching me slipping in it. I didn't know why Spank was still at the house, but if he came to talk about dog food I couldn't let Joyce hear it. Spank must not have received my text telling him not to show up, but I was glad he was here. I needed to let him know what was going on with me and what to look for. I prayed I had a picture of Omar in the house to give to him, so he could share it with Rico. The detectives didn't know my goons worked overtime for me, and Omar would be dead before they ever arrested his ass.

As I turned the key in the door, something didn't feel right. It was like my hand had gotten heavy, and it was hard for me to turn the knob. It felt like something was trying to stop me from going in, but I walked in anyway. There was a tall nigga standing in my bedroom door, but it wasn't Spank. Before I could try to make out who it was, he was on the floor.

Omar came running out of my room in my pajamas with a gun in his hand, and I rushed him. My body was in the fight I had waited all my life for, but not my mind. My thoughts were on Bria's crime scene pictures, the letter Sierra had written trying to clear me, and Uncle Leroy and me play fighting outside my store. This nigga had killed all three of them trying to get to me, and now I had his ass.

I threw punch after punch at his sunken-in face. Omar looked sick. He wasn't the Big O who had gotten carried out of my house three years ago. He was a skeletal version of himself. He must've had lost forty pounds since our last encounter, which made me wonder what he was doing in Detroit; and then the realization kicked in that I was fighting my brother. My punches slowed down, and that was all Omar needed to get a few powerful hits in. I had taken three hits to my head that should have put me to sleep, and I wasn't about to take a fourth. I wrapped my arms around him like boxers did to get a breather.

"You're tapping out already, Dee? I'm just getting started. Killing you is going to be easier than I expected."

He was talking shit about me being tired, but he was the one breathing hard. I did a quick assessment of his face to see what damage my punches had caused, but all I saw was a slightly busted lip.

"I'm not the one who's going to end up dead."

I let go of the hold I had on him only to free my right hand and give him two haymakers to the nose. The blood spraying from his nose had caught my attention, and I slept on the fact that I had freed his left arm. He hit me with an uppercut that not only made me fly back, it sent my teeth into my tongue.

Within seconds, the roles had changed, and Omar was on top. The blood from his nose dripped down on to my face as his hits restarted. He began drilling on me, and although I was hitting him back, my hits were only landing to the sides of his face. The faster he swung, the more his blood covered me. It was a blessing in disguise because his blood covered my face like baby oil, making his punches softer and less accurate. I wouldn't pretend that Omar's hits weren't sending me into a daze. He was hitting me so hard that I couldn't remember to swallow, and the blood in my mouth had built up. The only thing I could think about doing to save myself from the upcoming knockout was to spit it all into his face.

"You're a dirty motherfucka!" he yelled out and grabbed the bottom of the pajama shirt to clean his face. And like I had done so many times in the past, I took that opportunity to run. I didn't run like a track star. Instead, I scooted away from his reach on my butt to put some space in between us.

"Fuck you, Omar. You brought on all of this shit on yourself," I yelled back, wiping his blood off my face.

As he made it to his feet, I noticed that he staggered a little bit and gripped his side like he was in pain. I jumped to my feet, tucked my head, and started working on his body. Every time I hit him in his side, he let out an agonizing sound. He finally couldn't take anymore.

Chapter 15

Omar

Demarcus was a lot faster than me with throwing his punches. For every one I threw, he returned five. He had my nose leaking, and I didn't need an X-ray to know my shit was broken. I saw the punch coming and the force he put behind it was like a wrecking ball. I needed a break, but I knew he wasn't in the mood to give out one, so I connected an uppercut to his chin, and he fell back.

Like a lion in heat, I attacked his ass and went to work on him. No matter how hard I was hitting him, he looked unbothered. I didn't know I had done any damage to him until he spit a mouthful of blood into my face, blinding me. When I stood up to clean my face, I moved too fast on my still healing ribs, and Demarcus saw my weakness. He jumped to his feet and began working my ribs like a cow hanging on a string.

After three power hits to my side, I had to tap out.

"Nigga, you're really trying to kill me over that bitch?" I asked, stepping back until I felt the back of my slippers hit the wall. I leaned on the hallway's bathroom door where I had Spank's dead body behind it, soaking in the tub, and the door open some. I had forgotten to close it behind me when I grabbed the lotion.

"You wanted to kill me. This shit ain't about Bria."

"That's what your mouth says. Unc told me you wanted a sword fight over that ho."

"That must have been before you killed him," Demarcus yelled.

I couldn't do shit but laugh. Not at his accusation, but at the DVD still playing. Demarcus was asking Bria whose pussy was it and the lying bitch was screaming it was his. The DVD had caught Demarcus's attention too.

"I was checking out your flick before you interrupted. That bitch fucked and sucked me the same way." Demarcus took a step closer, but I stopped him in his tracks. "I thought you said this wasn't about her."

"It's not, but it is. That bitch was a ho, but you didn't have to kill her. You had already fucked up her life."

"You're talking about the dog food she was on? I didn't get the bitch addicted," I yelled. "She had been dipping in my supply," I lied.

Demarcus wasn't listening to me. His attention had moved past me to the bathroom. I turned around to see if he could see Spank from where he was standing, and when I looked back at him I was met by his fist. On impact, I fell to the floor, and he ran inside the bathroom and started screaming, "You killed Spank!"

I looked in the bathroom, and Demarcus had his hands in the tub freeing the water in it. I took that as my opportunity to grab the gun. I tried to stand up, but my ribs wouldn't allow it, so I crawled to it. As soon as I had it back in my hands, Demarcus came charging into the hallway with hell on his face.

"I wouldn't do that if I were you," I said, laughing, slumped on the floor.

Chapter 16

Demarcus

This nigga had killed Spank, and the last strings keeping my heart from breaking had torn. I snatched the plug out of the tub and pulled my homeboy up. Once I got him up, I closed his eyes and kissed him on the forehead. I was done talking to Omar. This nigga had to die.

I ran out the bathroom and found Omar lying on the floor with a gun in his hands. I wanted to rush him, but if I took one step closer he'd pull the trigger.

"So I guess this is it," I said, throwing my hands up. "You win."

"I always win, Demarcus. Bria told me, before I killed the bitch, that you never compared to me. That ho couldn't stop loving me no matter how hard she tried. Unc said you wanted to be like me bad, but damn, why'd you have to go after my wife? Did you really think you could take my girl?"

"I did one better than that. I started a family with your bitch. If she loved you so much, why did the ho have my son?" I was about to die, but I had to give him one last punch to the gut before I left this earth.

"Stop lying. You know what? That shit doesn't matter to me anyways because, if y'all do have a son, it'll be me raising him." He aimed the gun at my chest.

"I know. He'll be raised by his uncle Big O."

"What? What the fuck are you talking about now, Demarcus? Those hits I gave you to the head fucked you up," Omar said with a chuckle.

"I'm not fucked up. The detectives who are sitting outside looking for you told me. Better than that, they showed me the proof that we're brothers. I was fucked up when they said it, but the shit is true. My mama crept with your daddy. But that ain't the fucked-up part about it. What's fucked up is everybody in the family knew but me and you."

Omar lowered the gun but not on purpose. I took it he was trying to make sense out of the news I'd just given him. Tears came out of the corners of my eyes, and I said fuck it. "Okay, I'm ready to die, big bruh. Like you said, you always win."

He lifted the gun back up with confusion written all over his face. I wanted death to come expeditiously, but he still hadn't pulled the trigger. Outside the center of my gaze, I saw something black. It was hovering in the air, but I didn't recognize what it was until it hit Omar over his head. The nigga who had been lying on the ground was working Omar with my floor lamp. When he dropped the gun, I ran and picked it up. The silencer had come off, but I twisted it back on and aimed it from one person to the other. When the nigga saw I had it on him, he put the lamp down.

"Who in the fuck are you?"

He had been shot in the leg and in his side, but he looked far from death. "L'Amir. I tried to have Sierra reach you for me to tell you I was going to handle your problem. This nigga Omar killed my sister."

At his last words, he started kicking Omar with his boot, stomping on his ribs. Omar was screaming in pain and asking for me to help him. I couldn't believe what I was about to do.

"Stop kicking him!" I yelled.

He stopped instantaneously and looked at me like I had lost mind; and, for a second, I thought I did.

"Little bruh, shoot that nigga," Omar moaned. "I know you ain't lying about us being brothers. I heard my mom and pops arguing over that shit when I was little. I tried to figure out why my Mom Dukes kept telling my dad to go take care of his other son and why she was talking about you. I asked that lying bitch about it, and she said she was just mad and screaming shit."

He was on his stomach, army crawling on his elbows to me. Blood was still pouring from his nose but not as bad as it did at first.

"Dee, none of this shit would have gone down like this if I would have known. We would have rocked with Lord King together. Fuck that bitch Bria and that shit our folks pulled on us. Kill that nigga, and we'll leave this bitch together. You already know the police are looking for me, my body count high, but I ain't ready to go to jail. I need to spend some time making shit right with my little brother and my nephew."

I took a step closer to shorten his destination. The shit Omar was saying needed some violin music playing softly behind it. "Bruh, you're the only family I have left from that fucked-up bloodline—"

He cut me off. "I know, but we don't need them, Dee."

"You don't know. What I'm saying is, you're the only nigga stopping me from getting a new start."

I pulled the trigger and put one in his head and then I snapped off.

"That's for Spank," I said, putting one in the back of his head since he was now face-down on the carpet. I kicked him in the face. "That's for Unc."

And then I unloaded the clip into him for Bria and my motherless son. I kept pulling the trigger, but nothing came out. I dropped the gun and fell on the floor next to Omar's dead body.

L'Amir bent down and squeezed my shoulder tightly. "It's all over now, youngster."

He grabbed the gun, and I knew it was his turn to kill me as he changed the clip out in the gun. With my eyes open and locked on Omar's body, I forced myself to think of my mother's pretty face. She was the true cause of the fucked-up plate I was given to eat off of, but I couldn't stop loving and missing her. I was lost in my thoughts as Omar body's jerked from the rounds L'Amir was putting into him, and I didn't notice when Rawlings and Ryu came in shooting.

The Future

Chapter 17

Demarcus

Five Years Later

It was cold as fuck for a Memphis Christmas morning. There was ice on the windshield of my pickup truck, and it took forever for it to warm up, but I wasn't going to let it stop me. I had put this off long enough, and now that I was ready to open a new chapter in my life, I needed to make sure I closed the last one. I had drove down Poplar many times over the years but I made sure to turn off the street before I passed Memorial Park. I wasn't ready to face my past, but today, when I saw the sign, I couldn't help but to smile. If felt weird to be turning in to it, but in a good way I was at peace. I pulled out the map the administrative associate had e-mailed me the day before with all the locations marked on it. I went to the one that had the most meaning to me first.

Uncle Leroy's grave was to the right of my grandmother's, and my mother's was on her left. It was my first time visiting any of their graves, and it was long overdue. I didn't know if I was supposed to talk or what, but I didn't have the urge to say anything besides, "I love and miss all of you."

My words weren't deep, but I meant them all the same. I placed the flowers on each of their graves, kissed the pictures I had them put on their tombstones, and got back in the truck. Sierra's grave was the closest to theirs, so I jumped out the truck with it still running and placed the flowers and thank-you card I got her on it. Forgiveness worked in a strange away. Six years ago, if Sierra would have crossed my path, I would have killed her for putting me in jail, and now I was putting flowers on her grave, feeling like I was indebted to her.

"Excuse me, sir, but the cemetery isn't open yet," a female security officer said, meeting me at my truck.

"Merry Christmas," I said, reminding her of the day.

"I'm sorry. Merry Christmas, but I have to ask you to come back in an hour during normal operation times."

"Ma'am, I've been putting off the trip for five years. I'm scared that if I leave now I might not come back here." I dug in my pockets and pulled out $400 and handed it to her. "Can I leave my truck here and you take me around, please?"

She nodded her head but refused to take the money. "Sure, Mr. Elder. Hop in."

"Do I know you?" I asked, not remembering her cute yellow face.

"No, but I heard your motivational speech a few years ago in Atlanta. What you're doing for those boys is delightful," she said, making me smile.

We went to Aunt Cat's and her husband's—fuck it—my father's graves next, and I didn't have much to say besides apologizing to Aunt Cat for the hurt my mama caused her. I placed flowers on Big Omar's grave and two bundles on hers. I had little Omar buried on top of her. He wasn't in a casket, but I paid for him to be put in a nice urn with his initials engraved on it. To the rest of the world, L'Amir had killed him, but I knew the truth. After walking across a few graves, I made it to my father Lord King's grave. When I got there, I put the candle I had paid to be made on it. It said, TO MY REAL FATHER.

Keith was on one side, and my big brother Greg was on the other. Under that, it read, R.I.P. LORD KING AND GUTTA, THE LAST OF A DYING BREED.

I stayed at their graves the longest, and I noticed the security guard had left me to open up the rest of the gates. I had conquered my fear and closed that chapter of my life. I walked back to the car feeling good.

Before I pulled into my yard, I stopped in front of the trashcan. I snatched the linked chain off my neck that held some of Bria's ashes in it. Mrs. Roberts had had it made for me. I kissed it and then put it in the trash. There was no way I could move on to my future still carrying around the hurt from my past.

I hadn't closed the door before my son started up. "Please, Daddy. I promise I won't do a lot of running, and I'll take my asthma pump with me. They want me to play running back. Please, Daddy, please."

A'chance was pleading for me to let him go play football in the street with the other boys in the neighborhood once again. I didn't mind him playing, but his asthma was bad, and he hadn't finished opening his Christmas presents from what I could tell.

"Maybe a little later, A'chance. You still got a lot of presents to open."

"But they're out there playing now." He pouted.

I gave him the "no means no" look he had grown accustomed to, and then he said, "Yes, sir. Maybe later on." He was on the verge of tears.

"Let the boy be a boy, Demarcus. He's seven. He knows when he need to take a puff and chill out. Don't you, A'chance?" Mr. Roberts said, as always running to his great-nephew's defense.

"Yes, sir," A'chance said, smiling from ear to ear.

"Go ahead, but if you need a break take one; and no playing tackle," I said as he ran to the front the door.

"Daddy, we're playing in the street, and I'm too fast to get tackled anyways." He was out the door before I could say anything else.

"That boy is just like you and Bria. He's a fighter who knows those puppy dog eyes will get him his way. I see your neck is naked, too. Glad you handled what you needed to," Mr. Roberts said while waking Adam up. "Get up. You're going to sleep into the New Year."

"You don't understand how good it feels to be home from Iraq."

"But this isn't your home. You missed A'chance opening up your gift."

"Where is he? I bet he's upstairs playing his new video game now," Adam said, casing the room.

"Wrong. He's outside playing football with his friends," his dad told him.

"Shit, I'm going out there. I'm sure they need a quarterback."

Adam shot out the door, and I followed him. He joined A'chance's team, and I played quarterback against him. We were losing thanks to my son being unstoppable, but it felt good to be outside playing with him.

"Who's ready to eat?" Mrs. Roberts asked dressed like Mrs. Claus for the third year in a row. She was making it a tradition.

We ran in the house without answering, and she rushed us to the bathroom to wash up. The house smelled so good with the mixture of Christmas dinner and desserts in the air. They helped to cover up the smell of Mama Pfeiffer's weed smoke in the kitchen. I didn't allow smoking in the house because of my son's breathing problems, but weed is supposed to be a cure-all, and after all the years of arguing about it, we agreed the kitchen would be the only room she was allowed to smoke in as long as she was in there cooking.

Jaylan and Joseph Jr. arrived just in time to eat like their mama said they would. For the first time that we'd been spending the holidays together, they both came with female guests, filling our twelve-seat dining room table. Joyce thought I was crazy when I had it custom ordered, but now she saw why we needed it.

A'chance was the only child in the family, but if that ever changed I'd invest in a kids' table for the holidays. We prayed and then ate like pigs. The women had done their thing in the kitchen as always.

When we were done, all the men cleared the table and made preparations to watch the game in the den while the women did their thing in the living room, but it didn't go down as planned. Joyce started harping about A'chance opening his gifts as she passed out the ones she had brought for everyone in the house and telling them not to open them until A'chance was done. While my son was tearing through his gifts, our house phone rang. I answered it and immediately pressed one.

"Merry Christmas, my nigga," I screamed into the phone.

"Same to you and yours. What did Mama Pfeiffer cook?" It didn't surprise me that Rico was asking about food. He had spent one Christmas with us before he went to the federal penitentiary, and that was all it took for him to get hooked on Mama Pfeiffer's cooking. Rico had been in prison for the last three years. He got caught moving dog food from Texas to Memphis. He should have never been in the car knowing that he was running the city by himself, but his greedy ways hadn't changed. He was looking at thirteen years for this charge but, thanks to one of Joyce's friends, he got off with only having to serve five.

"You know she threw down." I laughed.

"I didn't call to speak to you, nigga. Put my nephew on the phone."

"A'chance," I yelled over the talk and laughter in the room. "Your uncle Rico wants to talk to you."

At the sound of Rico's name, the room shouted greetings of Merry Christmas to him and Joseph Jr. rushed to talk before A'chance took the phone. I didn't like the fact they had teamed up, but they were grown. As long as Joyce and I weren't in the middle of their shit, I didn't care what moves they made. I passed the phone and joined the family in the other room, holding the package Joyce had handed me but still had not allowed me to open. In a few minutes, JJ reentered the room.

"Now that everybody is here, except for A'chance, you can open your gifts," Joyce said, pushing her spiral curls out of her face. I still wasn't used to her not having dreads, but I understood her reasons for cutting them. She said she couldn't move to the next level with me with her dreads holding all her negative energy from her past. I'd get used to her curls as long as I didn't have to keep putting up with that ugly-ass wig she wore while hers grew back.

We tore into our gifts and Jaylen got his opened first.

"Greatest uncle in the world times two?" he said, holding his fake Oscar in the air.

It didn't take Mama Pfeiffer long to understand the symbolization of her gift. She was on her knees kissing her daughter's stomach before I realized I was about to be a daddy again.

The room was filled with cheers and hugs. A'chance came in the room, and Joyce told him the news.

"Daddy, telephone again," A'chance said, unbothered by the news given to him.

But I was bothered and still sitting in my chair. Yes, I had A'chance, but I didn't get custody of him until he was four. I had to take a series of classes to prove I was fit once the DNA test proved he was mine. Bria never told me she was pregnant, and all of this was new to me. I was happy about it but nervous at the same time.

Mr. Richards grabbed me my arm and pulled me out of the chair. "Go to her."

I went to her and scooped her off her feet. We kissed for two minutes, and then JJ interrupted us.

"Congrats, but the game is about to come on and I got money on it. There's still one gift left."

Everyone in the room looked at the empty tree. There wasn't anything under it besides ornaments that had fallen off of it.

"You smoke too much weed; there are no more gifts left," Jaylen said to his brother.

I had asked JJ to pick up a gift for me, but when I called the store it wasn't ready, so I didn't know what he was talking about.

"Demarcus, look at that ornament on the tree. It looks like a gift to me."

I snatched down the crystal ball he had put on the tree and I fell to one knee, shaking. The room went silent as I opened up the box. There were tiny letters engraved into the top that read, CONGRATULATIONS ON THE ENGAGEMENT, BUT RICO AND I FELT YOUR RING NEEDED AN UPGRADE.

I looked at JJ and smiled. He shot me a wink.

"Joyce, you said what you wouldn't accept me the way that I was when we met, and I made those changes. I did them for me and, in doing so, I learned that I don't want to spend a day without you. Next to A'chance and my new baby growing in your womb, you're my only reason for breathing. Will you do me the honor of becoming Mrs. Joyce Pfeiffer-Elder, Attorney at Law?" I said with a laugh.

She took my face into her hands and kissed me softly on the lips. "Before I answer, there's something I need to clear up because you definitely did look at your gift."

Jaylen ran to my box and opened it up. He pulled out a T-shirt that had a double ultrasound on it. One side of it said Baby A and the other read Baby B. On the back was an ultra sound picture of A'chance I had never seen with the words, FATHER OF THREE, over it.

"We're having twins?" I asked.

She nodded her head yes, and I damn near fainted, but A'chance reminded me I had a call waiting.

"Merry Christmas. This is Demarcus."

"Merry Christmas once again, Demarcus. Congratulations on the engagement and the twins as well. It sounds like I paid my debt to you just in time." The woman's voice could no longer conceal its accent. "Did you open the envelope I left on your front seat this morning when we met at the cemetery?"

"I wasn't aware that you had left anything in my truck this morning."

"Oh, yes. $250,000 should be enough payment for getting rid of the man who killed my last living relative."

"That wasn't me. It was—"

"Shush, don't do it. I hate liars, but I understand that we are on the phone, and it's Christmas. I'm sure you need to get back to your family. In the envelope, there's a round-trip ticket for you to meet with me January third. That's if you accept my job offer. If not, no hard feelings. My main concern was clearing my debt," she said with uncertainty in her voice.

"I'll check it out shortly, and who am I'm speaking with again? I'm sure the name on your security uniform didn't belong to you."

She laughed an old, tired woman's laugh, then said, "No, love, it didn't. Everyone calls me the queen, but I've learned to look at you like a long-distance relative for some odd reason. Our stories are the same, yet they are so different. You, my dear, can call me Melyssa."

The call disconnected before I could say anything else.

The End